## "The baby's safe. H

Another few steps. Rechecking the footprints, now every few inches, with drops of blood.

Liam often dreamed of meeting this woman he'd written so many letters to. Finding her dead would trample all he'd imagined.

Liam's flashlight landed on a hint of a white coat contrasted against the base of a broad tree. It bothered him to not see movement as his boots crunched through the light, powdery flakes. Her head was dropped to her chest, blood dripping onto her coat.

"Miss, can you hear me?"

No movement. His stomach clenched with dread. If this was who he genuinely thought it was, then she could not be dead.

Yanking off his glove, he reached between her bloodied mitten and coat sleeve, feeling for a pulse. The echo of her heartbeat fluttered against his fingertips.

She was alive.

"Ashlyn. Wake up."

A gunshot. The tree's bark fractured above his head. He grabbed the front of the woman's coat and pulled her down to the forest floor, covering her body with his.

**Jordyn Redwood** is a pediatric ER nurse by day, suspense novelist by night. She pursued her dream of becoming an author by first penning her medical thrillers *Proof, Poison* and *Peril.* Jordyn hosts *Redwood's Medical Edge*, a blog helping authors write medically accurate fiction. Living near the Rocky Mountains with her husband, two beautiful daughters and one crazy dog provides inspiration for her books. She loves to get email from her readers at jredwood1@gmail.com.

## Books by Jordyn Redwood

### Love Inspired Suspense

*Fractured Memory*
*Taken Hostage*
*Fugitive Spy*
*Christmas Baby Rescue*

Visit the Author Profile page at LoveInspired.com.

# CHRISTMAS BABY RESCUE

## JORDYN REDWOOD

**LOVE INSPIRED** SUSPENSE
INSPIRATIONAL ROMANCE

LOVE INSPIRED® SUSPENSE
INSPIRATIONAL ROMANCE

ISBN-13: 978-1-335-58814-2

Recycling programs
for this product may
not exist in your area.

Christmas Baby Rescue

For questions and comments about the quality of this book, please contact us at CustomerService@Harlequin.com.

Love Inspired
22 Adelaide St. West, 41st Floor
Toronto, Ontario M5H 4E3, Canada
www.LoveInspired.com

Printed in U.S.A.

In my Father's house are many mansions: if it were not so, I would have told you. I go to prepare a place for you.
—*John* 14:2

For Linda Mai.
I love sharing our writing journeys together.

# ONE

Liam Knight jolted awake, bathed in sweat. He sat up and reached for his loaded SIG Sauer, never more than an arm's length away, and double-checked it was in good working order. Every time he slept, the same nightmare occurred. Transported back to the Afghanistan battlefield, he tried to deactivate a bomb in a school building as an enemy soldier, weapon poised, drove straight at him. Liam raised his weapon in defense, and when he fired, the gun jammed. Fear would shoot through his unconsciousness, driving his eyes open. His heart raced, his breath coming in short puffs as if he'd been sprinting. Some referred to it as the warrior's dream.

For him, it was torture.

Doc Montgomery called it PTSD. Liam was loath to honor it with a name. That would give it power over his life, but something had to change. These dreams were having a cumulative negative effect. Without the structure of the military, he lacked direction and a goal. *What can I do with my life now?* He fingered his gold navy SEAL trident pin that had been next to his weapon. At that time, though dangerous, his life had been easier than facing this void of uncertainty, but the self-imposed isolation kept people safe from himself and the dissociative PTSD reactions he could have. He feared hurting people during flashbacks when his mind drifted from the present.

*Ultimately, it's better that I'm alone. Safer for everyone that way.*

A high-pitched whine howled outside, an empty confirmation of his statement, forcing tufts of Christmas Eve snow under his door.

This remote cabin, built by his hands, had been far from the warm, comforting welcome home that he craved, but it was a necessary prison where he sat in self-incriminating judgment that he would give a limb to forget.

There was a knock at the door. Faint—to the point he wondered if his imagination was playing tricks on him.

Liam stood, placing the weapon in the holster at his side, a habit unbroken from his years in the military. He tugged down the tails of the blue-and-gray flannel shirt to cover it. When he opened the door, the vastness of pine trees and snow filled his vision. He stepped out onto the porch when his boot knocked against something, and he looked down.

An infant carrier encased in a pastel, quilted cover that prevented him from seeing what was inside. Reflexively—and against all his training—he picked it up and then saw the set of footprints up to his porch and going away.

And the droplets of blood that shadowed them.

Instinctively, he stepped back inside his cabin, closed the door for cover and threw his back against the wall.

Then the infant fussed. His heartbeat raced. Crying children were a trigger for him that could precede a drift from reality. His vision grew fuzzy, and he felt the plastic handle slipping from the grip of his sweaty hand.

*Focus on the here and now. Feel your feet on the floor. The warmth of the fire. Your breath coming in and out of your chest.*

Liam threw the dead bolt on the door and carried the car seat near the fireplace burning bright with half-consumed logs. He sat on the worn leather couch, placing the carrier beside him, taking long, deep breaths to slow his pulse, as his mind sorted through the implications. He eased the coverlet down.

Sure enough, there was an infant strapped inside. A girl, if the pink clothing was a hint, her eyes wide and unblinking. For a moment, something softened inside him. An echo of what his life had been like before war and death. Her face scrunched, turning red, and her mouth opened to scream when he noticed the pacifier lying on her chest. He picked it up, placed it into her mouth, and she hungrily began sucking on it.

"Hey, there, little one," he said, as his hand gently rocked the carrier. "Seems like whoever brought you here might be in trouble." Her eyes pinned him, tugging noticeably at his heartstrings. He cut those invisible ties. He couldn't risk the emotional connection. It would pull him hard into a dark well of grief.

Who had brought her here? Had they left items to care for her outside that he hadn't seen? He slid his hand into the crevice between the baby and the side of the carrier. When he came up with nothing, he tried the other side.

His hands gripped a journal and an envelope.

With his name on it.

Writing he recognized.

If those words had been penned by the hand he knew, a woman who had been his military pen pal for the last several years, then he had to find her. If the blood was hers, then she could be dying or dead. Reading the note…investigating the journal…would have to wait.

He picked the carrier up and placed it on the

floor near the fireplace. "Stay warm. No noise." He placed a finger to his lips, attempting to give her a gentle but stern stare for compliance.

Liam paced to the door, grabbed his brown Bedale jacket and hustled into it. Next, he thrust his hands into a tight-fitting pair of gloves as he went through his well-rehearsed checklist. This was a mission, and he was going to prepare as usual. Leaning over, he patted through his jeans to his right midcalf to ensure the small revolver was still present—his jeans split at the seam for easy access. He wouldn't need much for the search, so he grabbed a flashlight and stepped out onto the porch, locking the door behind him. The person who'd brought him the infant wanted to protect her, and if he were heading up his own search party, the door would be the only thing between the baby and whoever intended harm.

Liam inhaled deeply, intentionally slowing his breathing to keep his pulse in check, as he popped the flashlight on and held it under his weapon. He took one step down and noticed a backpack that had fallen off the stoop. Likely supplies for the baby, but his training told him IED. Even unicorn backpacks held death in the Middle East. In his mind, nothing was innocent anymore. At the base of the steps, he gained a trajectory for the set of footprints. He scanned the pine trees, their boughs heavy with snow. A half-carved moon overhead provided additional light as he walked to the side of the indentations. What he would give for a pair of night vision goggles. After every three or four steps, he would stop, listen. The foot impressions and droplets of blood were spread farther apart, a sign the person had some speed in their retreat. Now he'd have to follow the small-size footsteps, presumably left by a woman, into more dense woods.

The forest was not as quiet as many believed. Listening, really listening, brought forth a rhythm, an inhalation-exhalation of life that never ceased and kept him grounded in reality. Clumps of snowflakes fell off trees with soft tufts into snowbanks. The flutter of wings as an owl took flight. The howl of a wolf returned with more in response from the pack. The crisp air laden with the scent of pine tingled in his nose and sharpened his senses.

The trail was a story of arrival and departure. The woman had kept the same path to and from his cabin. He wondered briefly how the infant was faring alone and chased the thought from his mind.

*Focus. Stay focused.*

Intermittently, next to the footprints, there were impressions in the snow where he suspected the woman had set the carrier down. There wasn't a car or remnants of tire tracks in the drive leading up to his cabin. How far had she trekked to find him? Had she chosen to walk through the woods to get away from someone tailing her?

Liam stopped. The snap of a branch, by something large, caused snow to shift and halted his motion. He rechecked the direction of the footprints with his flashlight. They were closer together here, where the woman had slowed her pace. She wasn't crying for help, another indication that she didn't want to be found. Whoever had injured her could still be in pursuit, which kept him from calling out to her.

Was she armed? Would she mistake him for someone who would harm her? After all, he was pointing a loaded gun. What woman would trust that? Sometimes, risks had to be taken, even if it seemed his own life could be altered by the choice. If the military had taught him one singular thing, it was that.

"The baby's safe," he said. Normal voice. Calm tone.

Another few steps. Stopping. Listening. Rechecking the footprints now intertwined as the path taken narrowed, now every few inches, with drops of blood.

"I won't hurt you. Help me find you."

It was as if his heartbeat had found hers and paired with it. The closer he came, the faster his rattled in his chest and the harder it was to keep his breath calm. He often dreamed of meeting this woman he'd written so many letters to. Finding her dead would trample all he'd imagined. When he briefly thought about a life different from what he was living, he often thought of her.

Liam's flashlight landed on a hint of a white coat contrasted against the base of a broad tree. The only thing that made it discernible from the snow was the ring of decorative fur around the hood. He was coming up behind her, and he started arcing around so as to not frighten her. It bothered him to see no movement as his boots crunched through the light, powdery flakes. He rounded to stand in front of her. Her head was dropped to her chest, blood dripping onto her coat, her feet outstretched, almost as if she had chosen to sit rather than slump down.

After holstering his gun, he reached forward and grabbed her hiking boot, shaking it. "Miss. Can you hear me?"

No movement. His stomach clenched with dread. If this was who he genuinely thought it was, then she could not be dead. It would mean God hadn't responded to his prayers to always keep her safe. The same prayer she always wrote to him in her notes.

Yanking off his glove, he reached between her bloodied mitten and coat sleeve, feeling for a pulse. Her skin was warm, and once his fingers found the right groove in her wrist, the echo of her heartbeat fluttered against his fingertips. He lifted one of his fingers and placed it under her nose. An exhaled breath warmed his skin.

She was alive.

The woman's long brown hair covered her face. On the left side of her head, the wisps matted with blood. Liam pulled the tendrils away from her face. Her eyes were closed. He gripped her shoulder. "Ashlyn. Wake up."

A gunshot. The tree's bark fractured above his head. He grabbed the front of the woman's coat and pulled her down to the forest floor, covering her body with his.

Pain and cold was all Ashlyn Sutton could register. Rescuing a baby from almost certain death and trying to get her to the one person she knew would keep her safe was her primary goal. She had done it. Secondarily, she wanted to solve her sister's murder. She was unlikely to accomplish that goal. Saving the child would preserve her sister's last imprint. Now, with the blood loss and her throbbing head, her thoughts came with almost silly randomness.

*Will Liam keep her safe? Was this the right choice? Lord, protect that sweet baby. She is all that can bring a guilty man to justice.*

A voice—his voice—had broken through the air. He'd come searching for her and found her. She attempted to lift a finger to her lips, to hush him—to protect him. She willed her thoughts to reach his mind.

*Please, don't try to rescue me. I'll be your death.*

The man who'd injured her was somewhere in this forest. She was sure of that.

Haziness followed. Clumsily, she wiped at the warm trickle of her blood as it traced its way down her neck. Her eyelids were heavy, and she didn't want to resist the lull of sleep anymore, her primary mission fulfilled. Then there was a tug at her boot. A finger at her wrist. A gentle hand on her head assessing her wound as he tried to keep his light from boring into her eyes. A voice came at her again, tunneled. Her ears still rang from the first time someone had shot her.

Then that same sound, again…

Suddenly, she was moving. The crisp air rushed against her face, not propelled by the wind but by the man's movements yanking her away from the tree. She rolled in his arms a few times, losing her mittens. Opening her eyes, she only saw the front of his coat, an American flag patch sewn there. He scanned the trees, one arm raised, the weapon in his hand, trying to find the source. Shifting his weight to the side, he groped through the inches of snow and found his flashlight. When he had it, he turned it off, severing the beacon the killer had used to find them.

"Don't move," he whispered.

She shivered. Even with the chill seeping into her bones, she felt safe—protected by this man she'd only written to but never met. Inherently, she trusted him. When she thought of family, she thought of him.

He lifted off her body. "I need to hide you."

What did that mean? It was dark. She was wearing a white coat, and there was snow to camouflage her presence. How easy could it be to find her, even in the moonlight? He sat on his haunches and pushed her underneath a large tree. The needles bristled against her face, the scent of pine reminiscent of Christmases not running away from a murderer. He reached down and pulled something from his ankle and wrapped her fingers around it. The hilt of a gun colder than her flesh. She shook her head and pushed it toward him.

"In case I can't find him in time." He nudged her arm back toward her chest. "The safety's off."

What good would this do her when she'd never touched one? He rose and was away. Ashlyn blinked several times, trying to clear the drops of blood that had strayed into her eyes. She looked up. The moonlight filtering through the tree branches was so similar to when she would lie under the Christmas tree as a child with her older sister. They would stay there for hours under the twinkling, colored lights, nestled among unopened presents, and would imagine what treasures lay within the boxes. Sometimes they were brave enough to pick them up and give them a gentle shake to see if they could garner any clues, before their foster mother would catch even the subtlest noise and admonish them for trying to peek.

Another gunshot. Ashlyn jerked. Was it true that you never heard the shot that killed you?

There was rustling, like animals fighting. Another gunshot. Ashlyn turned on her side. She crawled out from her hiding spot and sat up in time to see the man charging right at her, throwing his sniper rifle and brandishing a knife.

She raised the firearm and pulled the trigger. The kickback knocked her back into the tree. The man stumbled, but then raised himself up onto all fours. Liam tackled him from the side. Ashlyn scurried to a standing position, the adrenaline surge giving her the strength, and she pointed the gun at the man's head.

"Drop the knife or I'll shoot you again." Her voice was stronger and more determined than she felt as her stomach melted into her feet.

He raised his arms up and dropped the knife.

Liam stood up and brushed the snow from his legs. "Good shot."

It was hard to miss when the target was a foot away and bearing down.

She reached out to hand the weapon to Liam when her vision blurred. He took it from her. She rested her hands on her knees.

Keeping his gun trained on her would-be murderer, he stepped sideways to her. "Easy now. It's all right."

He grabbed at her elbow a moment too late, and she crashed into the snow. A cool blackness enveloped her.

# TWO

Liam paced with the baby, giving her a bottle as Doc Montgomery tended to Ashlyn in his bedroom. Thoughts mired his mind. What would the sheriff think about the man he'd tied up in the woods? What story was Liam going to tell him? The truth? Would it have been wiser to take Ashlyn to a hospital? Probably, but until he knew what this threat was against her, less public exposure was the more prudent option, in his opinion. The infant thrust the nipple from her mouth. He grabbed a cloth, laid it on his shoulder, set her on it and gently patted her back. He'd seen countless women use this technique and assumed it was the superior method, and before long, a soft burp escaped her lips. He nestled her back into his arms, and she reached forward and wrapped her fingers in his beard.

And yanked…hard. His eyes teared as he gently disentangled her fingers.

Liam noticed the satisfied smirk on her face.

"I hope that smile is because you're fed and not because you enjoyed a little trickery." As his father once said about women, they were mischievous from the outset. Maybe it was the one accurate piece of advice he'd ever uttered. Liam peered into her brown eyes, and there was something about the sweet innocence in them that made everything in his world slow down—captured by this one moment in time.

Sitting near the fireplace, Liam nestled her in the crevice between his legs and rocked her gently side to side. She kicked her legs and gurgled. Instantly, a smile echoed on his face and an unsurpassed feeling of joy touched him—if briefly. How could one little creature stir something that he had thought he would never feel again? Liam reached out a hand and she grasped his finger. It surprised him how comfortable he was with her. He hadn't been around babies much. Only rescued them and other children while serving in the military in villages where poverty and the iron fist of brutal tribal leaders were the norm. His failure on a military mission had cost two children their lives and for that he wouldn't forgive himself. After that, he'd pushed aside the idea of being a father himself. How could he entertain the thought when he had failed so miserably in the past to protect children from harm? He hadn't had a great example of a father growing up anyway, and if he modeled what he knew about parenting from his own family, then he wouldn't be all that nurturing.

The door to his bedroom opened and Doc Montgomery came out and sat next to him on the couch.

"You're a natural with her," Doc said.

"You know me taking care of a baby would never work," Liam said.

"How have your nightmares been lately?"

"Same. Worse. Better. Depends on the day," Liam said, refusing to look Doc's way. If he engaged in eye contact, the doctor's acute assessment skills would determine that was a lie.

"Mmm-hmm…" The doubt in Doc's vocalization was obvious. "She wants to see—"

"The baby, of course." Liam picked the infant up and handed her to the doctor.

"Just you for now," Doc said, gently rocking her in his arms. "Been a long time since I held something this small." He raised his eyes and caught Liam's. "I expect there will be a lot for you and me to talk about. About how it is you're really doing."

If Doc only knew the truth of those words. He was more nervous about having a conversation with this woman—Ashlyn—than he was holding the infant.

"How is she?"

"I'll let her tell you. Best that way."

As he faced the direction of his bedroom, a prolonged beep echoed from both their phones. Liam reached into his pocket and swiped his thumb over the glass.

An Amber Alert.

Liam read through the text. His heart rate edged up.

A female infant last seen with a woman by the name of Ashlyn Sutton. Please call Jackson Police Department with any information.

"Anything you want to tell me?" Doc arched his eyebrows.

Liam remained silent.

Doc continued, "Most injured women running with a child are trying to protect them. Right now, it's good enough for me that you trust her. Will you protect her? The baby? They're in trouble. I don't think she'd be here otherwise." He raked his fingers through his gray beard, his light blue eyes downcast. "Considering what she's been through, I'm not eager to involve anyone without knowing more of her story. You better go find out what we're dealing with."

Liam walked to his bedroom door, wiped his

palms on his jeans before grabbing the cool, scratched brass doorknob. He knocked twice with his free hand and pushed the door open once permission was granted.

Immediately, he was that high school boy approaching a girl he'd had a crush on for years. All the same feelings. Heart racing. Stomach hollow yet cramped. Dry mouth. The pictures she'd sent of herself did not do her justice. Even with smudges of dirt and blood on her face—pine needles entangled in her hair—she took his breath away. His hand braced against the door frame until he felt more balanced. Even before he'd seen her photo, it was her words that had helped heal some of the trauma of what he'd seen in the war but not spoken of.

Her words—accepting and empathetic—were a healing salve. Ashlyn was his safe place, but the distance between them, some of the anonymity of putting words on paper versus extolling them in public forums, made it easier for him to share the deepest parts of himself. It frightened him to meet in flesh the one person who knew the most about him—about the darkest places of his soul. Of course she'd bring the child to him—he'd never told her about the ones he'd lost.

After all that he'd disclosed, she'd still come here. Trusted him…for what?

*Is she disappointed? Is she wondering if she should have sought help from someone else?*

Liam shifted on his feet. Her eyes settled on him, and she smoothed the tattered log cabin quilt under her hands before she reached an arm out to him. "I'm Ashlyn Sutton. Your pen pal for the last three years."

Liam closed the distance and took her hand in his. Her grip was firm, but her skin soft as silk. "Liam Knight."

He pulled a wooden chair close to the bed, and she fiddled with the covers. There was a deep gash in her forehead that Doc had expertly stitched closed. The right side of her face, beneath the cut, had swelled and darkened in the well below her eye. Tomorrow, a shiner for sure.

"I always wondered how it would be the first time we met," she said, her voice deeper, sultrier than he'd imagined. There was assurance in her words. A self-confidence he liked. Much like her words on the page.

"I didn't imagine you'd leave a baby on my doorstep."

A faint smile played on her lips. "True. I never thought I'd do that, either. I wanted to investigate what happened to Mackenzie, and I knew Emory was safest with you."

"How are you feeling?" Liam asked.

Gingerly, she reached up and traced the cut

with her fingers. "Fourteen stitches, according to the doctor. Could have been much worse. I've got a screaming headache. Nauseated. Probably a concussion."

Liam knew the defense mechanism by heart. Rely on the knowledge. She was a nurse by trade, so it was easy for her to self-analyze her injuries, but that wasn't really what he was asking.

"I mean, how are you *really*." He placed his elbows on his thighs and leaned forward, reached out his hand and covered hers with his.

She bit her lip. Her green eyes tinged with chocolate-brown flecks glistened. "I'm in trouble. A lot of trouble."

Having a plan and pulling it off were two separate things. Ashlyn had a vision of Liam, but expectations tended to be disparate from reality. A disappointment when the fantasy met true-life circumstance. Had this been wise? To involve a man she only knew through the penning of letters across great distances? Her notes had followed him through all the places his military career had taken him over the last three years, and his voluntary discharge after serving his country for a decade.

Now, she knew she'd risked that her instincts about Liam were true, and she wasn't sure if her gut had been all that reliable in the past.

Besides, on paper, people typically presented a facade of their true selves.

"Trouble?" Liam prompted. "I gathered—"

"No, like I don't know if I'll live through what's happening."

"From your attempted murder, I assumed you weren't coming by to offer to take me to Disney or anything."

Humor as deflection. That was always a strong point for him in his letters. Self-deprecating. Humble. These were qualities she adored and rarely found in men she met. It was the reason she'd allowed her sister to convince her to seek a military pen pal as part of a new organization her sister's boyfriend had founded. Ashlyn wasn't looking for a physical fling. She wanted a connection with a man on an authentic level. Someone she could trust to be loyal. She had to know if that existed somewhere. The complications that were her life would always melt away when she read through his troubles and offered to help him see the other side. Her faith, her nursing skills—it felt like she was offering him a long-distance lifeline.

Now she needed him to help her see what she couldn't.

She inhaled and slowly exhaled through pursed lips to calm down the swarm of butterflies bumping against themselves inside her chest. There was the emotional connection they shared that was strong, and then there was the budding reality that his presence stirred in her, an intense physical chaos that she hadn't felt in a long time. He was taller than her by a good four inches. His face tan, even in winter, meant he spent hours outside. Longer than military-cut brown, wavy hair.

She gripped the sheets to mask the tremble in her hands.

"I don't mean to rush you," he said, drawing her attention back to his Nordic-blue eyes. "But until I understand the nature of the trouble that brought you here, I can't adequately protect you or the baby. There's an Amber Alert out for you."

A thickness developed at the base of her throat. She tried to swallow past it. She closed her eyes as the pain in her head intensified and her fingers pressed against her temple did little to abate it. The pain reliever Doc had given her wasn't cutting it.

Liam cleared his throat and brought her vision into focus. She took the water he offered. Their fingertips brushed slightly. The tingle lingered as she drank.

"I don't know where to start. How far back to go," Ashlyn said.

"One word at a time. Tell me whatever you think might be relevant."

"The baby is my niece. I was worried about my sister—have been worried for many months now."

"Why?"

"Her boyfriend… I think he hired someone to kill her."

"So she's…"

"Dead, yes. I was there visiting her when a man, someone I don't know, came to her home."

The words tumbled. She gripped the glass tighter.

So much of that night she had quarantined in her mind to stave off the terror. Now all the emotions bubbled from her, the pressure too much. A wail escaped her lips—the cry of despair she heard as a nurse only when the direst news was delivered. Her body shuddered, droplets of water spilled from the glass, and Liam took it from her before she dumped the contents onto his bed. She curled into herself, her hands covering her eyes, as the tremors shook every inch of her. Now that her survival was assured for the moment, the commotion of that night looked to escape the prison she'd locked it in.

To be so emotionally vulnerable with someone who was essentially a stranger increased her fear. What had she been thinking? What was he thinking?

*What a mess this woman is? How can I pos-*

*sibly help her? Where is the nearest phone so that I can call the police and get her out of my house?*

Then she felt his hand grip her shin through the covers. Just the right amount of pressure to spread a calming wave within her. No words—his touch spoke more volumes than his letters.

"I'm sorry," Liam offered.

Ashlyn wiped her cheeks free of tears and grabbed a tissue from the box on the nightstand, clearing the snot running down her face. Might as well let it all show. Then he'd know full well what he was getting into. What a disaster he was aligning himself with.

"Why do you believe her boyfriend wanted her dead?" Liam pressed.

"So many reasons, but mostly because of her baby."

"It's his?"

"Yes."

"And why would he want to kill the mother of his child?"

"Because it's not politically convenient that my niece is alive. He is married. A well-known politician running for governor—"

"Douglas Hughes?" Liam swallowed hard.

"You know him?" The question hung heavy in the air between them. Did Liam know Douglas? Would he tell her?

Liam shook his head. "It's not important. Why do you think he might have killed your sister?"

Ashlyn swallowed. He was hiding something. Maybe she was wrong to place trust in him. "Mackenzie wanted to use him, his political clout, to raise awareness and money for my niece's illness."

"The baby is sick?"

"Not now, but she will be…is. Emory was not my sister's first child. She had another before her…a son that had a genetic neuromuscular wasting disease. My sister's a carrier… It's complicated. Going public would have exposed their affair, even though he's not currently living with his wife. It would show he wasn't faithful when they were together."

"The son…was it Hughes's as well?"

"No, my sister and he met after her son's death. My sister kept pressuring Douglas about raising money for Emory's cure, and she was telling me she was going to force him to do as she asked."

"So Mackenzie's death would silence that. Do you think it was the intention to kill the baby as well?"

"I was elsewhere in the house when the man came inside. My sister went to the door to answer it. I went to the nursery to sit with my niece, who was starting to fuss. I figured that, whoever it was, I would leave them to their private conversation. I heard arguing…my sister screaming. I grabbed the baby and hid in her panic room for hours. There're cameras in there with full views of the outside of the house and many of the rooms inside."

"Why not call the police from the safe room?"

"Because Douglas is good friends with the chief of police."

# THREE

Even as Liam asked, he'd known what Ashlyn's answer would be.

What he hadn't disclosed in the moment of her question was that Douglas Hughes was Liam's half brother, older by nearly ten years. She was also correct that Douglas was close friends with Jackson police chief Wesley Taylor.

Douglas and Wesley had been allies for decades. Since Douglas's high school years. Liam's memories of the two were vivid. Both were bullies who'd taken it upon themselves to torment Liam at every opportunity. Constant pranks and beatings. Liam's experience from his youth made him want to fight for those who could not defend themselves. With an abusive father and alcoholic mother, no one seemed the wiser about the mistreatment Liam suffered. Douglas filled the power vacuum when their father was not present and, unfortunately, seemed to admire their father's undesirable traits. Liam knew his brother's desire to learn political acumen. When Douglas sought office, he'd badgered Liam relentlessly to use his war stories, the wounds he had suffered, to help raise money for his political campaigns. Douglas had created the military pen pal organization that had matched him and Ashlyn together. Did Douglas and Ashlyn's sister pair them intentionally, hoping to ignite an attraction? It would be great fodder for any political campaign. He'd agreed to be a pen pal initially to get Douglas off his back, but even doing that never seemed to be enough.

*Tell your story,* Douglas would beg him. *Help your brother. Let's do more for veterans. We can do so much together.*

Liam couldn't stomach it. He hadn't known Douglas had a woman on the side. That they'd had a baby together. That the child he'd held moments ago was his niece. His brother had lied, cheated and manipulated his way to every political victory he'd ever had. Loopholes were a legal means to cheat the system. But murder? Was it possible for Douglas to stoop so low?

They were both the sons of a violent man. Two different mothers. Douglas's mother had deserted him when he was a toddler, and it wasn't known if she was alive or dead. His brother touted how he'd overcome his past.

Douglas had two sons with his wife. The American dream of rising from the ashes, overcoming destitution and poverty to run for Wyoming governor and eventually the highest office in the land. He knew Doug wanted the US presidency. Would do anything to get there. Being a Wyoming state senator wasn't enough.

But murder with his own hands or being the mastermind behind it?

Was it possible?

"Do you think it was Douglas Hughes that showed up at your sister's door?"

"I didn't see. I heard the arguing, the gunshots, and hid with the baby. When I figured out how to turn on the cameras, the assailant was gone."

Ashlyn paused. Her eyes bored into his. "You know my sister's boyfriend? You've looked a light shade of green ever since you mentioned his name."

He'd never intentionally hidden anything from her. He didn't want to do it now. "He's my brother."

Before he could blink, further think through the repercussions of divulging this information, she was up out of the bed and clamoring for her bloody clothes. The gray-and-red flannel shirt of his that Doc had dressed her in was seemingly three sizes too big. She tilted to the side, likely light-headed from her head injury, and he reached out to steady her. She pushed his arm away.

"Where are you going?" Liam asked.

"I can't stay here."

"Why?"

Her eyes widened. "Your brother? Seriously? You never mention his name in three years of letters?"

Liam's stomach sank at her accusation. "*My half brother.* Older by nearly ten years. We're not close. He's a user. I decided a long time ago to not let my life be overshadowed by him. I'm not close to my family... You know this."

"It seems like something you would have shared." A tinge of anger in her words.

"Sometimes a person makes a choice to cut people out of their lives. People that aren't healthy for them, in order to live a sane existence. It's called setting boundaries."

"Or just another way to isolate yourself," Ashlyn charged. The truth—it stung.

Liam took a breath. The train was tilting off the tracks. He'd witnessed the beginning of enough fights to know a derailment when it was coming. He didn't want that with Ashlyn. "Not writing about him was my way of keeping Douglas out of my life. Revisiting my youth isn't helpful to me—it's very painful. I did not mean to deceive you. How could I have known there would ever be a connection like this between us?"

"You didn't know about my sister then? And their affair?"

"No, and you have written little about your sister."

Ashlyn sat back down on the bed and fingered the buttons of the shirt. His accusation stalled her sudden rush to change clothes. She looked everywhere in the room but at him and it broke him. Clearly, she needed help. Trusted him to help her enough to involve him in a murder mystery. If she discarded him in the first fifteen minutes of their meeting, who could she turn to? Maybe it was better that she learned now that she shouldn't depend on him to keep her or Emory safe.

He sat down next to her on the bed. "Do you know who's following you?"

Ashlyn shook her head and backhanded the tears off her cheeks. "I left with the baby in my sister's car so I didn't have to transfer the base for the infant carrier. Plus, it's in much better shape than mine and—"

"Where is the car?" Liam interrupted.

"Off the road about half a mile from your—"

"They're tracking the vehicle. It's the only way they could have followed you here. The movement of your sister's car would have been confusing to whoever oversaw carrying out this murder. If my brother is involved, he would never dirty his own hands. Do you have any idea who he would have turned to? Are you sure your sister has died?"

"I'm a nurse. I know fatal wounds when I see them. Why would you ask that?"

Wounds. As in more than one.

"Can I ask where they were?"

Ashlyn bit her lip. More tears flowed. She touched her heart and her forehead. "Blood in both places."

It spoke of a professional hit.

"Did you see her…body up close?"

"Through the live feed in the panic room I couldn't. I didn't know how to change the view or position them to see more clearly."

Liam grabbed another tissue and handed it to her.

From what Ashlyn's letters did share of family, her sister was her only sibling. They were raised in the foster care system. Liam and Ashlyn were both broken by their childhoods and trying to have a normal life. It was what bound them so deeply in their letters.

Their shared tragic pasts.

However, Liam used isolation to protect others from himself. He worried his PTSD reactions could be violent and he couldn't live with hurting or failing to rescue anyone again. Ashlyn longed for a permanent family, even if she had to create one for herself. He couldn't handle it if she were injured or worse.

If Douglas wanted to wipe out the potential revelation of his affair and of the child he'd fathered, he'd have to get rid of the baby as well. He'd have to also get rid of any witnesses to his crimes.

Would have to get rid of Ashlyn, too.

"What are you thinking?" Ashlyn asked.

"Why did the assailant give up on looking for the baby at the house? They are following you now. That is clear. To kill you both."

A shadow passed across the window. Liam pulled Ashlyn to the floor and killed the light on the nightstand. She dashed to the nearest wall and huddled there with her back against it.

"Stay here. Get your shoes on. I'm going to grab Doc and the baby."

He crawled to the door, staying below the level of the windows. When he opened the door, only the indistinct glow from flickering flames shed any light on the room. Liam dropped lower and shimmied into the living room. Doc was on the floor, too, the infant clutched to his chest. Both their old military instincts kicked in.

"I'm assuming you don't get many visitors," Montgomery said.

"You saw someone?" Liam whispered.

"A shadow across the window."

They were leaving—all of them—if they were going to stay alive. Liam grabbed the letter and journal and shoved them into the backpack that Ashlyn had left earlier, and their coats that still lay strewn over the back of the sofa. He tossed the doctor his and took the infant so Doc could put it on.

"How do you imagine we're going to get past this guy...or guys?"

"The tunnel."

"When was the last time you were through there?"

"A year, maybe more."

Liam motioned to the doctor to follow. It was difficult to crawl, holding an infant in one hand, but when they got back to his bedroom, Ashlyn had done as instructed.

He handed Emory back to Ashlyn. "We'll need to figure out a way to carry her so both your hands are free."

"How are we getting out of here?" Ashlyn asked.

"Old mine shaft. Our friend here built this cabin right on top of it," Doc answered. "We can make a swaddle using the bedsheet." He got up on his knees to pull the linens off the bed.

Liam saw the red laser light of death settle

on Doc's chest and he lunged from his position to drive him to the ground as the shot broke through the glass.

Cold sweat dusted Liam's body. His nerves zipped with adrenaline. Whoever was coming for Ashlyn and this baby would not stop.

Until all of them were dead.

Ashlyn's heart thumped wildly at the base of her throat as she clutched Emory to her chest. The noise of the gunshot was deceptively quiet, other than the light tinkling of glass shards as they showered into the room. Bitterly cold air followed in its wake.

The doctor was prone on the floor, apparently unharmed. He'd taken a knife out of his pocket and was cutting the sheet into something Ashlyn could use to carry Emory. He tossed her a large triangle section. She scooted to a corner of the bedroom that held more shelter from the window than her previous position. She set Emory down as she tied two ends of the fabric behind her neck and tucked her niece inside, placing the pacifier in her mouth, hoping that would keep her placated, quiet. The remaining ends she tied behind her back. Ashlyn rested a hand on Emory's back and tried to discern her breathing from her own rapid inhalations to ensure the wrap wasn't too tight. Liam opened his closet and grabbed a weathered satchel, throwing the strap over his head and under one arm, then shifted the pouch to his back. He rolled up the woodland area rug, exposing a door cut into the floor.

He heaved the hatch to the tunnel open. A plume of dust filtered up from the cavern. Underneath was a metal grate that he slid off to one side. A musty odor, a mix of deep earth and rotting leaves, wafted up through the room. From a shelf in the closet, Liam grabbed a couple of flashlights and handed one to Ashlyn and the doctor.

"What's keeping this person from following us?" Ashlyn asked. "From coming into the cabin?"

"I have a trick, but we have to move."

Dying in a tunnel underground. Gunned down as she escaped with a baby tied to her chest. Yesterday she was out having tea with friends. Now her sister was dead, and she was on the run. A fugitive.

Liam held her coat up and she slipped it on. The doctor was positioned on the ladder that led down. The icy wind through the window evaporated the sheen of fear that coated Ashlyn's skin. Her teeth chattered—from fear, from cold. A toss-up at this point.

"You have to go next," Liam ordered.

This was one of those moments where reality smacked her hard in the face. What choice did she have? Trust was a flimsy ideal when a gunman was on your tail. There was a large crack—like an ax hitting wood.

"He's coming," Liam said.

Ashlyn scooted on her bottom toward the hole. She could see the doctor below her, several rungs down on a rickety metal ladder.

"That will not hold both of us—all three of us," Ashlyn said, her voice shaky.

"It will, I promise. It's stronger than it looks. It will hold with you and Doc on it. When you two are at the bottom, I'll come down."

Ashlyn got on all fours. The baby held snug to her chest. Doc's hand reached up and grabbed her boot and pulled her foot until it rested on the ladder rung. Liam took both of her hands to hold her steady until both feet were secure. Her knees knocked as she scooted her feet down another rung. Now her body was waist level with the floor. She'd have to ease back to get Emory's body through the hole.

Another crack. The sound of wood splintering. Liam let go of one of her hands to pull a weapon from his side.

"Go, go, go!"

Ashlyn took two more steps down, her hands slippery on the chilled metal. If the room were any colder, her sweaty skin would have frozen to the bar. It was dark, only a faint hint of light coming up from Doc's flashlight. Descending the ladder was mostly by the feel of Doc's guiding hands. Finally, she felt her feet rest on dirt rather than metal.

"Liam! She's down."

Booms of gunfire echoed through the space. Ashlyn ducked. Doc grabbed her and guided her into a crevice as he turned off his flashlight. He pulled her down and the two of them huddled there. Ashlyn's eyes adjusted to the darkness and she finally saw a white slice of Liam's socks peeking from between his boots and jeans. He was fully on the ladder. The sound of bullets pinging against metal raked along Ashlyn's spine, her nerves like live wires. Liam jumped off the ladder onto the dirt and raced toward them.

"Whoever it is is in the bedroom. If he got through my front door, it will not take him long to get rid of the lock I put to secure the grate we came through to get into the tunnel. Let's move!"

Liam pulled her up onto jittery legs. He grabbed her elbow and broke into a slow jog. The doctor trailed them, his flashlight back on, helping to illuminate the darkness in front of them. Ashlyn stumbled the first few steps, clutching Emory to hold her steady. They turned right, a length of mine cart track in front of them. The flashlight beams danced against varying colors of brown and gray where miners had used pickaxes and carved wounds into the granite.

The tunnel was larger than she'd thought it would be. They could stand up.

More gunshots behind them. Rocks broke free from the wall as the bullets found purchase. Had their assailant made it through the grate? Another gunshot and Doc went down beside her.

"The doctor…he's down." Ashlyn pulled up.

Liam propelled her forward. "I've got him. Keep moving! Straight. Another two hundred yards."

She ran but didn't see what could help them in that distance.

Liam edged next to her, the Doc slung over his shoulder. "We're close."

Rocks splintered from the ceiling. Would the whole thing come down? How secure was this tunnel?

Liam stopped running and set Doc on the ground. Ashlyn knelt next to him and helped stem the bleeding from his thigh with two hands over the wound. He winced as she pressed. Liam reached into a breach in the wall. The sound was deafening as he pulled the heavy metal door over a set of tracks that would sever the gunman from their path and locked it into place.

"He will not get through that door, and he's not going to know where the tunnel's exit is. My cabin is far from where we'll see daylight. However, if he's got explosives, we better keep moving."

Ashlyn's breath caught in her chest. A shudder ran through her.

*Explosives? Who are these people?*

# FOUR

Christmas morning. Most families were waking up to a bright sun, the snow shimmering off its rays. As the smell of warm cinnamon rolls and hot chocolate filled homes, parents would be trying to stem the excitement of young children ready to tear through Christmas presents. Liam couldn't remember the last time he'd experienced a traditional celebration with presents and gifts and...happiness.

For himself and the three visitors to his cabin last night, the journey to safety had been rough. They were all exhausted from the adventure. It had taken hours to get through the tunnel with Doc unable to bear weight on his leg. Once out, Liam had insisted that Doc and Ashlyn rest in an unused hunting shed well hidden on his property. There was an old woodstove in the shed where he'd lit them a fire until he could get medical personnel to the area. The structure didn't have a road leading up to it, so EMS had to hike in and carry Doc out on a stretcher. Liam and Ashlyn walked behind the crew, Liam carrying Emory, until they got to a sheriff's vehicle.

Liam paced a small office outside the interrogation rooms of the Teton County Sheriff's Office. Sheriff Tom Black had found the suspect that Liam had left tied up in the woods and currently had him apprehended and contemplating his life choices. Cracking his knuckles as he viewed the suspect through the two-way mirror, Liam eyed the worn patch on the man's roughly discarded jacket on the chair next to him. The lion with a trident tail. At some point in time, they had been members of the same division, though they'd never crossed paths. At least, not that Liam remembered. Ashlyn was close in a nearby office with the door open, feeding Emory. An officer sat close, monitoring the two—there *was* an Amber Alert out for Emory—but Liam strayed glances now and then to verify Ashlyn was there…that she was real.

Doc Montgomery was at the ER getting his leg tended to. The bullet had broken his femur, and he was soon to go into surgery to get a rod placed. Black was discussing interview strategies with one of his underlings, and it was more than he could take.

"I want to talk to him," Liam said.

Sheriff Black rose and tossed his pen onto the desk. "Absolutely not. It would be highly irregular—career-ending for me would not be an overstatement."

"Then deputize me."

Black rolled his eyes. "Liam, you're a friend, but this is not in your wheelhouse. Yes, you're ex-military, but you're not trained in interrogation."

"I am, more than you know. Just not something I talk about."

Black scratched his fingers through his short, well-trimmed salt-and-pepper goatee. "We're not going to use military-style interrogation."

Liam folded his arms over his chest. "I'm not talking about that. He's not going to talk to you."

"And what makes you think he'll talk to *you*?"

"We served in the same unit," Liam said.

"You know him?"

Liam faced Black. "No, but I have a better chance of getting something out of him than you do. Have you formally arrested him yet?"

"Yes."

"He's been read his rights? Asked for a lawyer?"

"Of course, and surprisingly, no."

"Then just turn on your recording equipment and let me talk to him soldier to soldier."

"I'm in the room," Black insisted.

"Figured you'd want it that way."

"First sign of trouble and I'm booting you out."

"There won't be any." The words sounded insincere to Liam, and the questioning look Black gave him said the sheriff didn't believe him, either, but would take the risk. Nothing was worse for tourism during the Christmas season than a mercenary on the loose, and it was in Black's interest to get this issue closed out as quietly as possible. Maybe with the spirit of the season prominent, Black approved his request and swore him in as a temporary deputy for the length of the interview.

Liam kept his coat on so his own insignia would be easier for the man to see. In war, anything that could be used as an advantage was one. He hoped this man hadn't strayed too far from the military oaths he'd taken. That even if he'd chosen a criminal life, Liam could bring him back into the fold. Before entering the room, he checked on Ashlyn and the officer one more time. The deputy gave him a reassuring nod, though his confidence didn't soothe Liam's anxiety.

Liam entered the room behind the sheriff and took a seat at the interrogation table. The man set his cuffed wrists on top, and Liam got a close look at his hands and forearms. At one point in time, this man had imbibed everything military. His tattoos signaled honor and service. What had happened that caused him to go after an innocent woman and child?

"This is Liam Knight," Black said. Liam resisted the urge to reach out and shake his hand. "And what should we call you?"

The man shrugged. Liam sat at the table. The assailant had close-cut brown hair—shorter than military-style. His pigmented dark brown eyes were lackluster, a defeated cast clouded over them, almost as if washed over with watered-down chocolate milk. A few cuts and scrapes marred his face from his capture at Liam's hands, but he had far fewer injuries than Ashlyn or Doc had at this point.

The man's identity remained elusive. He'd been fingerprinted by the sheriff's office, and they were running the prints through the normal law enforcement databases. However, with the military, there had to be a name with those prints for verification. Only if he'd committed a crime before would he likely show up in civilian searches, and it wouldn't surprise Liam if that didn't happen. Whatever life he was leading, this was probably the first time law enforcement had shackled him.

"Did you serve overseas?" Liam asked, pointing to the patch on the jacket.

"More than enough times."

He looked perhaps ten years older than Liam's thirty-six years. "I served in Afghanistan," Liam offered.

The man jutted his chin. "I don't remember us crossing paths."

"Same. I'm just curious about what brought you to this point. Hunting down an innocent woman—an American that you're sworn to protect."

The man pulled his hands into his lap and eased back into the chair. "Money."

"I didn't think there was any amount of money that would entice an ex-SEAL to kill someone who wasn't a combatant."

"Then you haven't been in touch with many of our brethren."

Hyperbole. Had to be. Of course, there were rotten apples in every profession and Liam wasn't so naive as to think that each person who passed through the military ranks would always be upstanding.

"How much money?" Liam asked.

"More than I ever saw serving for Uncle Sam. Listen, you can be as hoity-toity as you want to be about my choices, but you haven't walked a day in my boots. I got bills to pay and I can't hold down a job…"

The man's voice trailed, and he broke Liam's gaze. Perhaps he and this former soldier weren't that far apart. Lots of vets had trouble holding down regular work after discharge. Liam could relate. Only because he'd saved up most of his money during his service years was he able to afford not to work. That didn't mean he didn't want to work—his psyche was currently keeping him from it.

"Same," Liam said.

The man lifted his eyes. They were glossy, but he pulled his eyebrows together—a determination not to cry. Or maybe a scowl. "Seems like you're getting off pretty well living in a swanky town like this one."

"I didn't spend my money on much other than investments when I was in the service, and I built the cabin I live in."

The man rubbed his cuffed hands over his face. The clinks of metal rattled with the motion. "Tristan Briar."

The sheriff nodded at the confession of his name.

There was a resignation in those words. Perhaps a crossroads Tristan had come to. What Liam hoped to achieve by participating in the interview might work.

"Listen," Tristan said. "You seem like a stand-up guy trying to make his way the right way in the world after all we've seen." He paused, rubbing his lips together and shaking his head up and down. The motion didn't prevent the tears from starting. He sniffed his nose hard. "I can't say the same. I *need* money. A lot. I just…couldn't adjust to things back home after what I…what we lived through, brother." The man backhanded his nose. "I got into drugs, which led to a lot of debt—not the good kind of debt. People are after me for the payout, so I looked for some easy options. A quick money grab that would solve my problems, which led me to some dark places on the internet. That's where I found the contract."

"Contract?" the sheriff asked.

"There is a contract posted on the dark web for her life. Extra if you take out the infant. Even I'm not that coldhearted." Tristan drummed his thumbs on the table. The clattering of the chains against the Formica rattled Liam's spine even more. "It's why I waited. I figured she was dropping off the baby to someone she knew— to keep it safe."

Liam cleared his throat—tight from the news just rendered. The man was lying. Maybe to protect himself from the truth. Ashlyn had been injured before she left the baby, so Tristan had clearly put Emory at risk. He decided to forgo pressing him on the moral turpitude. "The dark web, you said."

"A fitting name, if you ask me."

The sadness vanished, replaced by a casualness that turned Liam's stomach. Maybe it was a defense mechanism for Tristan to compartmentalize the emotion from the actions he'd taken. There were more than a few wayward soldiers, but Liam was thankful only a few turned away from their ideals, what they subscribed to in being part of the military, that they would consider such evil acts and talk about them like they were going out for ice cream. Tristan had been more emotional talking about his debt than murdering an innocent woman. The juxtaposition had a whiplash effect on Liam's thoughts.

"Is this the first contract you've carried out?" Black asked.

"I'm going to plead the Fifth on that one." Tristan leaned forward. "What you don't understand is that it won't be just one person after her. The contract goes up—there're going to be quite a few takers. Particularly for the amount of money they are awarding."

"How much?" Liam asked.

Tristan settled back again. Liam cringed at the smirk on his face. "One hundred thousand. May not seem like much for murder, but I can tell you it's one of the highest contracts open on the site by ten times. There's going to be a lot of interest."

He spoke as if discussing Black Friday shopping deals. "How do you get paid?"

"Provide proof of death. A photo of the kill and some sort of follow-up statement by the police confirming the demise. Contractors must be sure the target didn't take part with the hit man to fake the whole thing to split the money. Then payment fulfilled in cryptocurrency. Essentially untraceable."

"Targets have conspired with their hit man for the payout?" Black asked.

Tristan raised an eyebrow, which made Liam think he'd been involved in such a plot before. Maybe that was why he needed a ton of money quickly. Liam gripped his knees. Heat plumed in his chest. At the beginning of their conversation, he had a lot of sympathy for Tristan as a fellow vet. Now Liam wanted to reach across the table and strangle him.

"Can the contract be taken down? And if it can be—will people stop coming after her?" Liam asked.

"Only two ways people will stop coming after her and the little one. She dies, or the original poster rescinds the contract."

"How can we find out who that is?" Liam asked.

"Your guess is as good as mine. Other than electronic money, the only other currency that reigns higher on the dark web is anonymity. The poster has a screen name—OpDeathandDestruction. That's all I know." Tristan laced his fingers together and cracked his knuckles. "I'll tell you this last thing—they will not stop until one of those two things happens, and it doesn't matter where she is. Where the baby is. You'd be downright delusional if you think she's safe even here."

"Are you able to see this OpDeathand-Destruction's other contracts?" Liam asked.

"Sure."

"Did you see any contract on his account for a woman named Mackenzie?" Black followed.

"I didn't," Tristan said.

"Does that mean it was fulfilled?" Liam asked.

"Likely no. Those will stay up marked fulfilled with proof. If you suspect one was put out on this woman Mackenzie, and you can't find it, it could have been removed by the poster. No way to know until you find the person... alive or dead."

It was nearing noon on Christmas Day. Ashlyn cradled Emory in her arms with tears flowing down her cheeks. Her heart was rife with worry. The sheriff had notified Jackson Police of her and Emory's whereabouts because of the Amber Alert. Would they force her to give Emory to Douglas? Was there any way Ashlyn could prevent that?

Ashlyn wiped the tears free. The officer next

to her busied himself with paperwork. Liam and the sheriff had been in with the attacker from the woods for the last hour. Her body ached. She and the baby needed sleep. When could that happen? Every cell in her body felt weighed down with an extra ten pounds—a heaviness she couldn't shake off.

"Do you mind if we lie down on the floor?" Ashlyn asked.

"Be my guest. I'd offer you a couch, but the floor might be more comfortable. Let me see if I can scrounge up a blanket and a pillow."

The officer stood as Ashlyn eased to the ground. Booming sounds filled the room, followed by explosions of tinkling glass. Someone was outside shooting into the building. The officer was knocked off his feet and landed with a thud on his back. Something wet sprayed Ashlyn's face. She reached up. The droplets were thick. The smell of copper filled her nose.

Blood.

More gunfire. Too many shots for Ashlyn to count.

Liam and Sheriff Black rushed out of the interrogation room.

A gunshot punctured the drywall between them.

"Everyone down!" Black yelled as simultaneously he and Liam hit the floor.

Ashlyn sheltered Emory under the officer's desk. Hopefully, it would be enough to protect her. Her hands shook as she crawled across the floor to the downed officer. Liam was by her side in seconds.

"Where's Emory?"

Ashlyn pointed a shaky finger at the space underneath the desk. Liam nodded and gave her a thumbs-up. The officer's eyes were open, but his breaths came in panicked gulps. There was blood spatter on his face but no pool of blood underneath his body. As Ashlyn tore open his shirt, she could see the round splayed in his vest, but it looked like another hit near his armpit. Foamy blood bubbled up from the wound. Ashlyn clasped her hand over it. A switch flipped in her mind.

"You're going to be okay," Ashlyn reassured him. "Slow your breathing down."

The man shook his head and closed his eyes, his face tense with worry.

Five more shots came through the window. Ashlyn dropped lower, her left hand resting on the officer's wound, her mind willing the rest of her body to melt into the floor. To be invisible.

*Almighty Father in Heaven—we need You right now to protect us from this evil.*

Her words were interrupted by more gunfire.

Two additional officers poured into the office space, securing the door behind them.

Radio chatter filled the small space. The sheriff ordered the building locked down. Ashlyn didn't want to lift her head, but she had to do more to help the officer out. Glancing behind her, she saw the roll of Scotch tape on the desk.

Liam and Black crawled to a heavy-duty metal cabinet. Black handed Liam his service weapon and Liam headed toward the window.

"Can't see anyone," Liam hollered back.

Black removed two long guns from the case and threw one back at Liam. "We're going to need reinforcements if they've gotten inside the building. Someone to outflank them. Jackson Police are on their way because of the Amber Alert, but they may not be sending enough officers."

Which meant they were presuming more than one shooter.

Liam nodded. Ashlyn took the break in the gunfire to grab the roll of tape and the pair of scissors from the top of the desk. She pulled Emory's backpack with her as she headed back to her patient.

As usual in an emergency, her attention became razor focused. The sound of the sirens was dull in her ears. She cut a smaller square from one of the burping cloths and smeared some antibiotic ointment she had stocked in the bag on one side. She placed that side with the ointment against the chest wound and taped the improvised dressing down on three sides. This would allow air to escape but prevent further collapse of the officer's lung.

It was a temporary measure. They didn't design transparent tape to hold on to a hairy, shock-sweaty chest and Ashlyn had to keep reinforcing the sides to keep them in place.

More sirens. The sound of glass shattering. Voices yelling.

Ashlyn positioned herself prone on the ground, facing Emory, who was now crying under the desk. She placed her hand on the officer's chest to keep track of his breathing. Short, quickened breaths fluttered her hand up and down.

Electrical zips shot through Ashlyn's body. She bit her lip to keep from crying. If the people after her would attack a police station, then there really wasn't anywhere that she could be safe.

Not even Liam could protect her. No one could.

Ashlyn lifted her head as much as she dared and saw Liam and Sheriff Black standing shoulder to shoulder, firing round after round into the parking lot. Suddenly, they both stopped, with weapons remaining at their shoulders—looking and scanning. The sheriff gripped Liam's shoulder and he lowered his weapon. The Jackson Police had arrived.

Easing up on all fours, Ashlyn looked at the injured officer's face. His lips were tinged blue. Liam walked toward her, knelt and reached for Emory, pulling her from underneath the desk and wrapping her in his arms. His two hands enveloped her body as he held her close, shushing her cries with calming words. Ashlyn's heart stalled a smidgen with jealousy as she wished briefly for those arms to wrap around her. She chided herself for her ridiculous thoughts and returned her attention to the injured deputy, Carter Anderson—according to the blood-spattered name placard. Sheriff Black had grabbed an office-grade first aid kit and now knelt next to her.

"Nothing in that box is going to help him," Ashlyn said. "He needs an ambulance. Gunshot wound to the chest. Likely collapsed lung on the left side."

He nodded and stood, speaking into his radio. Liam rubbed the back of Emory's sweaty head. A deputy hustled two uniformed Jackson officers toward them, tailed by a man with a highly decorated jacket and his chest puffed out to match. He rounded into the room and locked eyes with Liam.

"Why would I not have guessed you'd tangle yourself in a mess like this." He squared his shoulders, hands gripped to his duty belt, and glowered at Ashlyn. "And looks like we found our kidnapped infant."

Sheriff Black positioned himself between Ashlyn and Jackson police chief Wesley Taylor. "Before you shoot your mouth off without knowing their side of the story, we're going to evacuate this injured officer and take it from there."

Liam turned his back and walked out of the room with Emory.

# FIVE

Liam clenched his hands so hard they were aching. He could have gone his whole life without encountering Jackson police chief Wesley Taylor, but here they were, facing off again. He felt like he'd traveled back to his school days. Why was it that the blemish of this bully's taunts in his life never left him? Why were those feelings so easily accessible? Feelings of being different, pushed around? Even joining the military to erase those impressions by doing something good hadn't vanquished the impact of this man's actions on his life.

Would he ever be free of those thoughts? Of his sense of failure?

The injured deputy had been taken to the local ER that was seeing more business from gunshot wounds in one twenty-four-hour period than in an average hunting season. He'd even heard Ashlyn ask if she could be of help since they were so overrun. Doc was out of surgery for the leg trauma, and word was that the deputy was being life-flighted out to the nearest Level I trauma center but was expected to live.

What Liam knew and how he was going to set his plan into motion were two separate things. Being in a public location had not proved ideal, and he struggled to think of somewhere he considered safe. The cabin was exposed, but he needed to get back there in the short term to gather supplies for what they needed to do.

They'd have to unravel this mystery on their own. He and Ashlyn would be better off independent of law enforcement. They could move more quickly. Adjust the game plan at the drop of a pin—or the sound of a gunshot. Currently, they were static targets and being closer to public institutions made them more visible. If Liam knew anything about Chief Wesley Taylor, it was that his hunger for media attention, like Liam's brother Douglas's, outweighed rational thought most of the time.

Ashlyn sat in a chair next to him holding Emory. She'd finally gone back to sleep after a bottle and some gentle nursery songs sung to her. Liam didn't feel good about keeping Emory with them. It was too dangerous. They were less mobile with a baby, but he didn't know if he could convince Ashlyn to let someone else keep an eye on her.

That was if Chief Taylor didn't lock them up and take Emory away anyway.

"The murder attempt that occurred at Liam's cabin and the one here are in my jurisdiction," Black argued to Taylor. The two of them were standing on the other side of the table, squared off like two bucks. Liam considered stopping the whole thing and asking for a lawyer, but that would just slow down him and Ashlyn being released. What could they charge the two of them with? As far as Liam understood it, protecting someone from a contract killer was not against the law.

"I have a missing woman on my hands, and she knows something about it!" Taylor yelled, pointing an accusatory finger in Ashlyn's direction. "She sits right here with the child we're looking for based on the Amber Alert."

Liam placed an arm over her shoulders and felt her muscles tense as she pulled Emory closer. Taylor's face reddened. He wasn't used to anyone opposing him or his command.

Liam's mind raced back to what Ashlyn had told him last night.

"What are you going to do, Wesley?" Black yelled. "Arrest her for fleeing an active crime scene and saving a baby's life when she thought she saw her sister murdered? Ashlyn is the baby's next of kin and Emory needs to stay with her for now. I don't think you'd like the media showing you taking this infant away from the only family she knows."

Liam put his hands up. "Both of you, stop! You're both speaking of two different crimes." As much as he hated to, he turned to Wesley Taylor. "You didn't find Mackenzie's body at her home?" In his peripheral vision, he saw every ounce of Ashlyn still as if flash-frozen by Jack Frost's breath.

"No body. No trace of her," Taylor confirmed. "Douglas reported Mackenzie and Emory missing. Said he went to her place—found blood in the entryway. He reviewed the tapes and knew Ashlyn was on the property and had taken Emory. That's when the Amber Alert was issued." Taylor turned his attention to Ashlyn. "She's not the baby's next of kin. Technically, she should go to Douglas, who is her father."

Liam smiled…more snark than kindness. "Douglas is ready for everyone in town to know about his affair? What do you think that would do for his run for governor? You might want to clear that with him and his public information officer before you travel down that road."

Checkmate.

Wesley visibly withered. So much had been said in that statement. That Taylor, as much as he wanted to believe it, didn't have agency over his own life. He answered to Douglas—always. Taylor was merely a leech holding on for hopes of something bigger if Douglas ever reached his political goals.

Taylor clenched his hand at his side, his face flushed, not able to focus on anyone. "I saved all your hides from those two gunmen, and this is the thanks I get! You're not…they're not going to help solve my crime?"

"I'm willing to answer questions, but Emory needs to stay with me and Liam," Ashlyn said. "It's obvious that the more public we are, the more easily we'll be found by these men."

Taylor yanked a chair back from the table and took a seat. "Why doesn't everyone in the room explain to me their side of things and I'll decide from there."

Liam cleared his throat. "I don't know why you're looking at Ashlyn as a suspect when it seems you should take a hard look at my brother. Don't statistics bear out that women are killed by a paramour—particularly one that's trying to hide a secret?"

Taylor mashed his lips together. "Are you accusing me of something, Liam? It seems you're implying that I'd be willing to help Douglas cover up a crime? We technically don't know what's happened to Mackenzie."

"I'm just asking the obvious. Have you questioned my brother in relation to Mackenzie going missing and the events that caused Ashlyn to flee her home with Emory? Have you asked him if he put the contract out on Ashlyn and Emory?"

Black scratched at his throat—eyeing Liam with glowering disapproval like a mother trying to get her child to behave themselves, without uttering a word. It would not work. There was too much hostility between the two men for a chastising look to break down years of torment.

"This is the first I've heard of any contract." Taylor turned to Black. "Have you verified that such a contract exists?"

Black cleared his throat. "We've hardly had time. It was during our interrogation of the first suspect that we even realized the possibility, before another two delinquents shot up the station. We have a screen name to investigate. That's about it."

"Have you talked to Douglas?" Liam asked again.

"Right now, he's not answering questions," Taylor confessed. "He's hired a lawyer."

Ashlyn woke up just as the sun was setting to find Liam stoking the fire. At some point, he'd layered blankets over her and Emory, and she was so exhausted she hadn't even realized it. It was late afternoon by the time the trio had returned to the cabin under the watchful eye of law enforcement. There was a sheriff's deputy stationed at the end of Liam's driveway and two posted out front. Liam felt they were safe for the moment until they could develop a plan. Before she had fallen asleep, Liam was resting on the floor beside them, one hand on Emory's back, almost to reassure himself that she was breathing. The other hand rested on the floor with a gun.

Ashlyn sat up. Emory stirred. Liam stood and walked to the kitchen. Ashlyn watched as he prepared a bottle and set it in a pan of warm water.

"I've been thinking about something," Liam said.

Ashlyn remained silent.

"I'm not convinced Mackenzie is dead," he followed.

Ashlyn gripped Emory tighter. "What's your theory?"

"There's no proof of it. People who operate on these dark websites like to boast about their crimes and there's no evidence thus far of Mackenzie's murder or an active contract. Only that she's missing."

"Then where is she?" Ashlyn asked. "She would never leave Emory willingly."

"That's the ultimate question. This has all got to be connected. Even if someone wanted to kill Mackenzie, why come after you and Emory? I guess as potential witnesses, but they didn't see you, so how do they know about you? What happened wasn't random. I think something didn't go according to plan."

"Then how do we go about finding her?" Ashlyn asked.

"We need to first talk to the person who statistically is most likely to be involved. Douglas." Before he approached, he dotted his wrist with the fluid from the bottle to test the temperature. "She must be hungry for dinner."

His thoughtfulness touched Ashlyn. It was unusual for someone who wasn't yet a father to be intuitive about a baby's needs. Ashlyn positioned Emory to take the bottle. Liam sat next to her and reached a hand out to Emory, and she grabbed it like a lifeline.

Ashlyn's stomach fluttered. This was everything she wanted coming to life under the worst possible circumstances. A dream, unfortunately tainted by reality. None of these things were hers. Emory wasn't her child. Liam wasn't her husband.

"Do you ever hope life could be like this every day?" Ashlyn asked.

"Being hunted down?"

"No, of course not! I mean the simplicity of home and family."

He rubbed his face with his hands and scratched at his beard. Would he want to have a family?

"It's not something I considered to be part of my future. Why would I want to repeat the mistakes of the past?"

*Lord, I'm not sure why You've brought us together under these terrible circumstances. I pray You protect us from this evil. Let Mackenzie be alive. Keep her safe. I pray for the recovery of Deputy Anderson and Doc Montgomery. That You would bring them quickly back to health. That You would help Liam and me out of this mess and bring the people responsible for these crimes to justice.*

"What are you thinking about?" Liam asked.

Her sadness at his statement—that was the truth. Was it so different, saying what was on her mind versus writing her innermost thoughts and feelings on a piece of paper? There was more intimacy speaking face-to-face, being in another's presence. Being with Liam was different, but it felt like it was something that would have naturally happened all along.

Too soon to confess to a man she was dreaming of a family with children, with him included. Especially when he had made such a declaration.

"I was thinking that it is still Christmas Day, and we should celebrate."

Liam chuckled. "You don't think I've prepared enough for Christmas?"

"Well, the utter lack of decorations would imply that you intended on not celebrating. However, what is that delicious smell?"

"I don't know about you, but I'm starving. I made a quick batch of chili and corn bread. Not a traditional Christmas dinner, but something."

Ashlyn's stomach growled. One of her favorite meals. She couldn't remember the last time she had a good batch of chili. It was hard cooking something like that when feeding one person.

"Do you own any Christmas decorations?" Ashlyn asked.

"A few. An artificial tree, and I think I can scrounge up some lights."

"Here in the forest and you've never cut a real tree?"

"To be honest, I haven't celebrated Christmas in years. Just didn't..." He turned from her and stood. He took his fingers and rubbed the inner part of his eye—Ashlyn felt like blocking an errant tear.

"I'm not about to let you go back out into

those woods and find a tree after what happened last night," he said.

He left her. Emory finished the bottle. Not too soon after, he pulled a five-foot artificial tree near the fireplace and unpacked a few boxes of lights and another small container filled with ornaments.

"I haven't opened these boxes in over a decade. No telling what's in there. I need to go put some plywood up over the window in the bedroom and clean the glass up. You and Emory can sleep in there tonight and I'll take the couch."

Ashlyn nodded. Everything about his body language suggested he needed to break away from her. Build a wall to hide whatever emotion he was feeling. She decided not to press him.

Standing from the couch, she folded the quilt that had covered them, placed it on the floor and set Emory on it with a rattle and a ball. The tree was sparse, having lost quite a few of its artificial needles. She found an old wooden crate and set the tree on top of it. Adding to its height would make it easier to decorate and hopefully more luminous for the space once the lights were in place. She opened the three light boxes and connected the strings together. Once she plugged the string in for a cursory check of function, Emory let out peals of laughter and reached her hand out to touch the lights. Ashlyn wrapped them around the tree, already feeling her spirit lighten. She grabbed the box of ornaments, first brushing the dust off the lid, and then lifted the top.

What she expected were store-bought bulbs. What she found was a treasure of Liam's past. Ornaments made by a child's hand at school to give as presents to a parent. Each contained a photo by grade. She set them side by side and got a good view of him as he aged—at least through middle school. Once a towheaded blond to a brown-haired, blue-eyed child. His yearly school picture encased in different ways—in the belly of a reindeer, in the middle of a snow globe. His hand traced to look like a turkey. There were also homemade Christmas ornaments, likely crafted by Liam's mother before she abandoned her family. Styrofoam spheres covered in remnants of fabric. The same fabric from quilts she recognized scattered throughout Liam's home. She compared one ball to the starry quilt Liam had brought to the couch and found several matching fabrics. There were beaded snowflake ornaments as well. Despite Liam's mother's alcoholism, she'd taken the time and energy to make these handmade heirlooms, and it made Ashlyn want to know more about the woman she was before liquor became her escape. She'd been resourceful. After Ashlyn finished, she dimmed the living room lights and lit a few candles she also found scattered around Liam's cabin. He'd kept them likely for something more resourceful than setting a mood.

She found an old box of ornament hooks and made quick work of placing all the items from the boxes. Pounding came from the bedroom. The sound of a vacuum. Perhaps an hour passed before Liam came back.

He let out a low whistle.

"You did all this in an hour?"

Ashlyn scooped Emory up from the floor. "Do you like it?"

Liam nodded, his eyes glassy in the candlelight. "We should eat. I'm starving."

Ashlyn's heart faltered at the absence of a genuine answer to her question. There was something there. A memory that haunted him and that he wasn't quite ready to deal with yet.

*Don't rush him. He'll open up when he's ready.*

They ate in silence—not exactly comfortably. Liam seemed focused on the tree to where he could barely make eye contact with her.

"Tell me about the history of some of those ornaments," Ashlyn said. "Who made them?"

Liam gathered up the dishes. "My mom... before she left."

His voice hitched as he turned to take the

dishes to the sink. She picked up Emory, who had been playing on the floor, and stood next to him, placing a hand on his arm. "Let me take care of these. Emory is probably tired of looking at my face. Why don't you sit with her? She loves to look at the tree."

Liam sank his hands deeper into the soapy water. "That's okay. I'm used to doing things on my own."

Ashlyn gripped his arm harder. "I know, but you're not alone anymore. I'm here with you. I want to be here with you. We can share these things together. You've helped me a lot in just one day. You've…saved my life and Emory's. The least I can do is let you rest for a moment."

Liam flicked the water off his hands and dried them. "It's so strange to hear you say those words. I can't remember the last time anyone outside the military offered to help me." Emory seemed excited about the change of pace and, as Liam scooped her up, she fisted her hands in his beard. "I have got to think about trimming this thing before she does some major damage."

"Seems like Doc has been helpful to you," Ashlyn said.

"That is true. I guess I meant…a woman."

He nestled Emory in his arms and headed toward the tree, sitting close to it, letting Emory reach out and play with the branches. Ashlyn rifled through the kitchen looking for the ingredients for hot chocolate but didn't find them. There were enough spices, milk and some black tea that she could make a decent chai. While the mixture boiled, she finished the dishes and scrubbed down the kitchen. Liam was a surprisingly clean chef and there wasn't much to do.

Ashlyn poured her chai concoction into two cups and headed toward the tree. She turned off the lights as she entered the living room, leaving the room awash in the glow of candlelight and the illumination from the Christmas tree.

He had positioned Emory under the tree to look up at the halo of lights. She giggled and kicked at the branches. Ashlyn handed Liam a cup and settled into a seated position next to him.

"What's this?" Liam asked, blowing the steam from the cup.

"Since I couldn't find any hot chocolate, I made chai. Not a coffee drinker, I take it?"

Liam smiled. "It amazes people how I lasted through my military years and didn't get addicted to it."

"I'm sure it's possible with black tea as well. People can become addicted to anything, it seems."

Liam nodded. A conversation brewed in his eyes—almost as if he was fighting with himself on whether he should share what he was thinking. He took a sip of the liquid. "Wow. This is amazing. I always shied away from trying chai, but now I think I found my new drink."

Ashlyn's heart warmed. These were the moments she always dreamed of having. The safety of a home with a loyal helpmate. Children. Simplicity. "This is what I've always loved about Christmas."

"A Charlie Brown Christmas tree with some dusty lights?" Liam chuckled. He meant it as a joke but it sounded like confession.

"The basics of Christmas. What it really means. The beginning of the ultimate sacrifice."

"How did you celebrate?" Liam asked.

Ashlyn sipped her drink, letting the spices mull over her tongue, giving her a moment to think through her response. Growing up in foster care had been a chaotic existence. It was never known how long you would be in one place. How long it would take a family to tire of the children and insist they move on. There were good people, of course, that provided these services to children, but what lacked was the commitment that came through adoption. Security wasn't something that existed through most of her upbringing, and it was something that Ashlyn wanted deep in her core.

"Since I could never depend on getting presents, I focused on things I could guarantee would be part of every celebration. There was usually a fun treat—a handful of candy, at least. Most families consistently would put up lights, so I would pull my sister under the tree to look at them."

Ashlyn set her cup to the side and motioned for Liam to do the same. She eased down onto her back and scooted so they sandwiched Emory in between them. Emory giggled and turned to Liam, sinking her fingers into his beard.

"This little one is like a heat-seeking missile with those fingers and my beard," he said, laughing as he pried her fingers from the coarse hair.

Ashlyn looked up into the boughs of the tree, trying to imagine the scent of pine a real tree would bring. An artificial tree was good for some things, but it was the scent she loved the most.

"Even though I had my sister with me, I felt this hollowness around Christmas especially. I was always jealous of the other kids. They would want to talk about the presents under the tree, but I would always ask them who was coming over for dinner. They would name a list of cousins, aunts, uncles and grandparents. I would create pictures of these people in my mind and crave to sit at that table and listen to their stories."

"I can see why you'd want that experience, but family isn't always what it's cracked up to be."

"What was Christmas like for you growing up?" Ashlyn asked.

Liam gnawed on his lower lip. "When I was young, little, it was good." He reached up and fingered some of the ornaments. "It was normal. I had at one time all those things you wished for." He dropped his hand down. "As I grew older, it wasn't like it should be. There was fighting. Even though you don't have the best memories, I'd almost trade them for what I experienced. Looking back as an adult, I know the real meaning of Christmas isn't supposed to be about presents, but for a kid, it equals that. So many times, one or the other withheld gifts as retaliation for the other person in the relationship—but it felt like punishment for us. It's hard to distill out adult actions and what they mean as a child when all you feel is hurt."

"At its most basic, Christmas is about giving. A sacrificial gift." Ashlyn turned on her side and faced him. "I'm sorry that was your experience, but I know you tried to make things better for other children. By giving up your time and safety to help children in war-torn countries."

"It was never enough. I think about them all the time. The people I tried to help—especially the kids. And now I'm plagued with wondering if they're even alive."

Ashlyn reached out and settled her hand over

his, surprised when he intertwined his fingers through hers and tightened them. When Ashlyn didn't know the right things to say, she often would reach out physically to the hurting person. Maybe it was a trait she honed as a nurse or something more inherent that her profession brought out. While she was here with Liam and Emory, for the briefest moment, everything seemed right in the world. If she could make the world stop, she could see herself being happy for the rest of her life.

"I did read through the Bible you sent me. I didn't feel very connected to the passages. How can your faith be so strong?" Liam asked.

Faith was such a nebulous thing. It wasn't something that could be taken down from a shelf and scrutinized, measured, felt tangibly. It had everything to do with connection and trust. That was one thing she loved about God. He was always there. Always present. Through creation. Through the Word. In relationship with other people.

"I just came to know God as the one thing I could depend on. I could talk to Him whenever I wanted to. How I survived I would call nothing less than miraculous. In moments like this, with you, I know God is real."

"I don't feel like I can ever be that way. I'm too…broken by my past. By the things I've seen."

"We're all broken, Liam."

"I'm just not sure my brokenness can be healed."

"Jesus didn't come for those that had it all together. He came for you and for me. He came for the broken."

Ashlyn closed her eyes and moved her hand up over Liam's heart—feeling the soft, steady beat under her palm. *Lord, You know this man as deeply as any other. You know that the pieces he considers irreparably broken can be put back together. That in You he can be made whole again. Lord, help Liam see that in You all things are possible if he can trust that opening himself up to that possibility is safer than living in his loneliness.*

# SIX

Liam awoke to the sound of his automatic coffee maker. He had one in stock for guests who never came. Perhaps he kept it in expectation that someday his self-imposed isolation would come to an end, and he'd be more open to sitting on his front porch, enjoying the sunrise with a cup of joe and a friend. He sat up to notice the distinctive lack of a coffee smell and wondered what Ashlyn had prepared for the morning.

Liam rubbed his hands over his face to chase away any remnants of sleep when a mild panic set in. He patted the bottom of his leg and felt the revolver still there. He hadn't set it on the table as he normally did. He'd slept…peacefully. The first night in probably one thousand sleeps where he hadn't been terrorized by vestiges of memories replayed by his subconscious in fitful rehashings of his failings.

He felt calm. Having something ready for him to drink in the morning made him feel cared for.

Liam eased back on the couch, looking at the tree decorated by Ashlyn's hands. It was simple but extravagant in the same measure. The twinkle lights gleamed. Somewhere, she'd found construction paper and made fine garlands from it. Not the chunky type stapled together by clumsy, sugar-cookie-buttered, kindergarten hands. She'd even made strings of popcorn garland. It was sweet and all the things a Christmas tree should be.

Homey.

The tree lights faded in the room as the sun burst through the windows. He checked his watch. Eight solid hours of slumber. He couldn't remember the last time any such thing had happened without the help of medication, which he shied away from.

There was a brisk knock at the door. Ashlyn and Emory remained cocooned in his bedroom. He hadn't heard a peep from Emory yet and did not know if she'd been up through the night.

Liam slipped into his boots and headed toward the door. He peeked out through the window to see Sheriff Black standing there. He opened the door and motioned him in.

"Glad to see you and my deputies are still alive," Black said.

"Same," Liam said as Black came inside. A light snow fell—dry and dusty. Black tapped his cowboy hat against his leg to shake the crystals loose.

"How's your injured deputy doing?" Liam asked.

"He'll make it," Black answered. "Garden hose in his chest for a few days for a collapsed lung, but he's awake and talking, which is a good thing. No damage to his heart that they can find, but the bullet came mighty close to it."

"That's good news. Can I get you something to drink?"

"Coffee?" Black asked.

"Not sure what Ashlyn brewed but it will be warm." Liam headed into the kitchen. It looked like simple black tea. He poured a cup for the sheriff and offered milk and sugar, which Black agreed to. Liam poured himself a cup and motioned him to sit at the small kitchen table.

The sheriff's eyes were dark, his forehead tensed. The man had not slept as easily as Liam.

"You're not safe here," Black said.

"I know," Liam said.

"I mean not in the city at all." Black smoothed his hand over his face. "I was happy to protect you here for one night, but considering all that's happened and the crimes we're investigating, I don't have the resources to cover normal operations, let alone 911 calls, at this point."

"You can pull your deputies. It's okay. I'll figure something out."

Black took a sip of his drink and placed his

elbows on the table. "It's more than that, Liam. I can't tell you how many calls for suspicious activity came through dispatch last night. This whole town is on edge. This is not your normal Christmas merriment with a sprinkle of tourists running amok. Dangerous people are pouring onto our streets and they're all looking to collect a bounty. I've never seen anything like it."

"I guess in desperate times people will do anything for a hundred thousand dollars."

That was the amount of the contract on Ashlyn's life.

"No, Liam. Not all people. Evil people. That's who's coming after you. Cockroaches that you would not think twice about dispatching. They operate on the fringes of society and only come to light when something like this tempts them."

"I hear you, but we're not going to be safe anywhere. We need to stay in the area to solve the mystery. Are you kicking me out of town?"

"Of course not. But you need to ensure the infant is somewhere safe."

"I've already thought about that."

"And you and Ashlyn need to stay mobile. Don't stay in the same place every night."

"It's not my first rodeo, Sheriff. I know how to hide from bad people."

"You can't come back here to the cabin.

Hopefully, this place will still stand by the time you get everything sorted out."

Liam glanced around. That statement pierced his heart. He was unexpectedly emotional about losing the one physical habitat that had kept him anchored. If it burned to the ground, what would he do then? There would be no haven.

"I can get the feds involved," Black said. "They're already sniffing around the attack at the sheriff's station. Want me to clue them in?"

"No—I don't want to talk to them. I don't need them. As far as what happened here, treat it like any other instance of trespassing. You and Wesley Taylor can fight over the rest and play nice with the feds. You know he'll want to do anything that will shine his star."

"Are you talking about Wesley Taylor or your brother?" Black asked.

"Both."

"I can keep one deputy stationed outside until noon today for you to work out a plan, but then you're on your own."

"Understood."

Black sipped the last remnant of his drink. "I'll do what I can for you, Liam, but it's probably not much. You two stay safe and hopefully we'll see each other on the other side when this is all over."

Black walked through the front door just as Ashlyn emerged with Emory in her arms.

"What's happening?" she asked.

"Time to move."

Ashlyn gripped Emory to her chest as she cried. What Liam was asking was impossible for her heart to accept. They sat in his SUV out in front of Doc Montgomery's house. All of Emory's things that Ashlyn had carried with her were packed in the back seat. Liam had explained the plan and started the process, but Ashlyn was reticent to agree.

"We can't keep her with us," Liam said.

Ashlyn shivered and pulled Emory tighter. Emory let out a soft whimper. Children were tactile creatures. She knew the baby was picking up on every bit of her distress, and it was causing her to fuss. She bounced her up and down in her arms.

"They'll take good care of her. Doc's wife has been pining for grandbabies for nearly a decade, and a couple of buddies of Doc's who are ex-military are going to stay with them. His house is like a fortress."

"If anything happens to her, I'll never forgive myself. She's all I have left of my sister."

"If she's with us, it's more likely she won't—"

"What…come out alive?"

Liam turned in his seat to face her. Her green eyes were rimmed with red. She looked out the passenger window. He placed his hand on her shoulder and stroked it. "Hopefully, it's just for a few days until this is all over."

"Or until we are dead. Then what happens to Emory? She goes to your heartless brother?"

"We can only deal with the problem in front of us, and right now, it's keeping this little one safe. If you have other ideas, I'm open to them."

No one Ashlyn could think of could protect Emory like someone who was ex-military. What could a couple of nurses do?

Liam took her silence as acceptance and exited the car. The tightness in her throat made it hard for her to breathe. Emory placed her chubby hands on Ashlyn's cheeks and leaned in—touching her lips to hers. It was the way infants showed affection. All messy and slobbery, and it made Ashlyn cry harder.

Liam opened the door and helped her stand. She felt shaky. Her head still ached, though it was better than the day before. Walking was easier, and she followed him down the cobblestoned path to a heavy wooden gate. He pressed an intercom and announced their arrival.

Liam was right. What Liam's cabin offered in its solitude, Doc's house offered in amenities suitably aligned with a small fortress. Likely, his hyperawareness after the Vietnam War had led him to such extremes for him to feel safe.

As they walked along the path, Ashlyn eyed the cameras in the trees. Liam said Doc's friends had set trip wires around the property to alarm if people were trying to sneak onto the ten-acre property. A small creek flowed nearby. At any other time, Ashlyn would have loved to sit in one of the Adirondack chairs with a cup of hot chocolate and a quilt and just sit in silence.

The front door was a heavy, ornately carved wooden masterpiece with Northwoods creatures cut into the grain. When it opened, Doc's wife beamed at them. She was about the same height as Ashlyn, with smartly styled short gray hair and washed-out blue eyes that spoke of wisdom earned and overflowing compassion. She immediately embraced Ashlyn in a hug. "Come in! Come in. I'm Dolores. I've got everything ready for our little guest."

Dolores's warm spirit was a salve to Ashlyn's soul. So much of the past forty-eight hours had been pure terror. Now it was like sunshine piercing through storm clouds. She placed her hand to the small of Ashlyn's back and guided her over the gray marbled floor and to the curved wooden staircase with a wrought iron railing just to the left of the foyer. The home was a palatial log cabin estate. When they crested the stairs, there was a long hallway with several offshoots. Dolores guided her down the second hallway to the right, which ended in a cove with a room. When Ashlyn stepped over the threshold, it was everything she wanted as a sanctuary for a child, and she stilled to take it all in.

A crib. A shelf lined with picture books. A padded rocking chair with ottoman right next to the window with a view of the small creek. Dolores worked the backpack off her shoulder, and Ashlyn shifted Emory to the other arm.

"Why don't you two sit for a minute while I go through these things to make sure I have everything I need to care for this little one... Emory, right?"

Ashlyn nodded, and she stepped slowly to the chair. The room was painted in a soft forest green—almost as if Dolores wanted to be prepared for the sex of any future grandchild. There was a white chenille coverlet next to the chair. As Ashlyn sat down, Dolores draped the blanket over her legs. "You look downright chilled."

From the weather or fear? Ashlyn couldn't ascertain the culprit.

"Thank you," Ashlyn said, her voice tight with emotion. If only she'd experienced a drop of this woman's kindness when she was growing up, her childhood would have been immensely better. Above all costs, she had to ensure that Emory grew up knowing warmth, kindness and safety. It had to ooze from her pores like it did from this woman's gentle soul.

Ashlyn wiped a trailing tear. She could tell Dolores was giving her a few moments to collect herself as she took inventory of the backpack contents and put them away in a dresser that contained a changing table on top.

"Doc said Emory was eight months old. I hope you don't mind. I thought you'd be short on clothes, considering the adventure you've been forced into, so I bought a few things. I want you to take them when you leave."

From the dresser, Dolores pulled outfit after outfit. Darling Christmas dresses and outfits. Enough pajamas where Emory could wear a new one every night for two weeks. All the things Ashlyn would have picked out for her little girl. All the things that Mackenzie would have, too. She turned back to the dresser. "Looks like I picked the same formula that you're using as well."

Ashlyn nested her hands behind Emory's back, trying to engage the little girl's eyes with hers, but Emory was too distracted by her new surroundings to give Ashlyn any mind. Ashlyn wanted to drink in every bit of this child in case…well, truth be told, in case she never saw her again.

"I can't thank you enough for watching after

her, considering the level of danger," Ashlyn said. "Are you sure it will not be too much trouble? Caring for Doc on top of it?"

"This place is like a mini military base camp. It might look like a log cabin on the outside, but it's built like a fort. There were some things that Doc couldn't leave behind when he left the military, even though he never served in combat. Seeing the resultant injuries—he always prepares for the worst-case scenario. I've just learned to live with that. And you also must know as a nurse yourself that medical people make the worst patients. He'll hardly let me lift a hand to help him. He thinks that helping with Emory will keep me out of his hair." Dolores neared her and pulled up another chair. "I'm sure Liam is much the same way—always preparing for the worst."

"I really only know Liam through his letters. From the short time I've spent with him, it seems like he's mostly hiding from life."

"I'm sure the last forty-eight hours have given you much more insight into the man than you realize. Can I see if she'll come to me?" Dolores reached her arms out and Emory happily complied, pushing at Ashlyn's arms for release.

Ashlyn leaned forward and relinquished her. It felt briefly like a moment of betrayal. Emory snuggled right into the woman's arms. Dolores reached next to her and grabbed a basket of toys, and offered several to Emory, who happily began playing with them.

Ashlyn thought about Dolores's statement. She had learned a lot about Liam in their short time together. That she could trust him to keep her safe. That he seemed in it for the long haul. What she didn't know was if the long haul for him was just getting her through this crisis. Ensuring to solve the mystery of who had put out the contract on her life. Past that, she didn't know what he thought and was scared to ask him. He seemed determined to listen to his psyche lecture him that his faults were permanent and could not be overcome.

The point was that all humans failed on some level, and real wholeness could only be achieved with God's help. It was clear Liam struggled with that sentiment.

"Looks like I'd need to cash out our bank account for all the thoughts I see running through those eyes of yours."

"How well do you know Liam?" Ashlyn asked.

"Probably not as well as I should. He's been a close friend of Doc's for years, but I've never had many one-on-one conversations with him."

"Does Doc ever talk to you much about his time in the military?"

"Some, but I also know there's a lot he keeps hidden for his own sanity. Dredging it up for him can bring about untold psychological distress, so I don't pressure him and try not to press him for more information when he does open up."

"I think Liam has almost…locked himself away from the thought of being with another person. He believes that living in isolation is the best way to protect others from himself."

"You feel there's a different reason?"

"Liam says he's too broken to be with someone."

"Do you want to be with Liam?"

Ashlyn avoided her gaze and settled her eyes on the river…drinking in the calming swirls and ripples. The soft cascades of waters sliding over smoothed rocks were a solace to the heart rate she was trying to temper. "*I want* to be with him. I felt very close to him through our letters, and his actions to help me are further proof he's the honorable man I hoped he would be."

Dolores turned Emory toward Ashlyn and snuggled her against her chest. "I sense some hesitation there."

"You can't force someone into a relationship. And even if Liam has feelings for me, which I'm not sure of, he could choose to protect himself versus risking his heart to love someone else."

"When Doc came back from overseas, there were pieces of him he left there. Pieces of his mind, his sanity and his heart."

"How did your relationship survive?" Ashlyn asked.

"For one, at our wedding, we promised one another to never utter the word *divorce*. That, regardless of our feelings, we were in it as we vowed, until death do us part. Two is time. The times we hurt one another can be mended, but it takes more than platitudes. It also takes risking your heart to know that true forgiveness is the one thing that brings the greatest reward."

Assuming both lived long enough to realize such a prospect.

Liam eyed Doc's casted leg. "How's it feeling?"

"Painful. Nothing I can't handle with some over-the-counter pain reliever."

Liam raised an eyebrow. "Sure about that? You move half an inch and you're wincing. I'm sure they gave you something stronger."

Doc waved off Liam's statement and declined to answer the question. "How is it I make it all the way through Nam and I'm one evening with you and take a bullet to the leg and get a broken femur?"

"I'm trying to keep you young and make sure your life stays full of adventure."

"Let me tell you, I don't need or want any more exploits. I'm trying to keep my last days as uneventful as possible."

Liam nodded. Doc had been an ever-present stabilizing force in his life. Other than Ashlyn's letters, he was the only other anchor.

"So, how have you been?" Doc asked.

"Other than running for my life…okay."

"I have seen little of you until very recently," Doc countered.

"It's winter and I don't like to be out in it."

"You and I both know that's not true. You've been isolating yourself more. Not returning my calls or emails."

"Sometimes it's just easier…being alone."

"I think that's a lie you've been telling yourself all this time, Liam, but at its heart I don't think you believe it."

"What makes you say that?"

"You've been writing letters to a woman for three years. That doesn't speak of someone who wants to be alone. I think what has you on edge are your feelings. From what you've shared, you've been falling for her over her words. You talk about her more than you realize. And now that she's here in the flesh…even an old man like me can see the attraction you have for her."

"Maybe."

"Not maybe…like certainty. You can't take

your eyes off her. Every move, I can see the worry in your eyes. That little Emory, along with Ashlyn, is tapping into something you thought was long buried. The opportunity of becoming part of a family—of being a father. You might say otherwise, but your actions prove you're open to the possibility. Unfortunately, you're worried that your demons won't let you have a calm and safe life with her. That she'll always be in danger."

"She will be if Douglas has his way."

"I didn't mean from him… *I meant from you.*"

Liam swallowed hard—his voice tight. "Won't she, though?"

"Liam, you can get treatment for your PTSD if you would just reach out. You don't have to continue to live with the nightmares and flash-backs. You can stay connected and grounded to reality, but you must do the work. Why won't you? I've never seen you shy away from a mission in your entire life, but for this one thing… you hide literally and figuratively, and I'm worried that the more you let this go on, it will be harder to correct course. You might make choices you'll end up regretting in the end."

Nothing like Doc to drive a dagger right into the heart of the issue. If it was just Ashlyn, he would probably take the risk of diving into the issues that plagued him. He could bring himself through the maddening adventure of sorting out this war in his mind for the prospect of the two of them being together.

The problem was Emory. Her presence was doing two things to him. One, it made him realize how much he loved children. How great he could be with them and how tempting it was to think about having them in his life...particularly if he and Ashlyn were on the journey together. Watching Ashlyn with Emory, how tender she was toward her, how intuitively she thought and cared for her every little need, and how fiercely she wanted to protect her, pulled the same out in Liam. Seeing the world through Emory's eyes free of the destruction he saw, but lit up in the wonder of newness unabated by evil, was healing for Liam. In the same breath, being with Emory reminded him of failing those small children when they needed someone most.

*When they needed him.*

He didn't think he could ever fail a child again and live through it.

"Do you believe in God, Doc?"

"Couldn't make it through the day without Him."

"Ashlyn has this strong, unabated faith. She sees God everywhere and I just don't. Not after everything…not after praying for innocent lives to be spared and my prayer went unanswered."

"You and I are warriors at heart. We are called to a special mission. Whether you think that's a divine calling or not is up to you to piece out. I can't speak to your feelings of a God who is distant. Who won't answer prayers. But I know it's harder to hear His voice if you're not connected to Him every day."

"Not sure I have time to think about all things God at the moment. The mission right now is to survive the contract that's on Ashlyn's life."

But the truth was…he was thinking about Ashlyn's words. About what she said about Christmas. How hope came in the smallest, most innocent of things to build a bridge back to a God that the world had become severed from. That He fixed brokenness.

It was the hardest, simplest, most amazing mystery, if true.

Doc's words pulled his attention back. "You'll survive this—I know. It might be the most difficult thing you've ever done, but you will come through the other end. What is on the other end, Liam? Your cabin and you looking at four walls thinking that the world without you is a better place? It's a lie you've sold yourself. All of us would like to see you more. You have so much to offer…not only to me as your friend but also to Ashlyn and Emory. However, you have to do the work to be there for her. Not just in the protective sense, which is a default mode for you, but on an emotional level, too."

"How did you do it? Overcome the things you saw to build this?"

"I had to risk feeling the loss of my mistakes. It was…painful. But I was also with someone who I knew would never leave me, so there was safety there, too."

"I'm not sure Ashlyn could take that."

"Don't sell her short. From what I can see, she might be the very woman you need who could work through that type of pain with you. I'm sure you've shared some of your experiences through your letters and she still showed up at your door."

Liam gritted his teeth. That statement was accurate mostly, but he had never shared with Ashlyn his darkest moment. The one that clung to him like a stench that could not be washed away.

And if she knew that…she would surely never stay.

# SEVEN

Liam gripped Ashlyn's hand as they made their way through the swarm of police that littered Douglas's lawn. The timing wasn't great to have a conversation like the one Liam was going to press, but this was also probably the safest place for him and Ashlyn. The heavy presence of law enforcement should prevent an attack in the short term.

Then he remembered the police station and hustled Ashlyn through the front door.

They were first met by an officer who took their names and information. Liam pulled Ashlyn through several corridors before they came to a large, theater-style television room.

Douglas sat on the couch, *Top Gun* playing on the screen, a tumbler of brown liquid at his side. If liquor, more than a single serving. He held a red card with his name scrolled on the outside. Not a card sent through the mail. Liam released Ashlyn's hand and walked next to the couch, hitting Mute on the remote control.

His brother turned, made eye contact and turned back to the screen with vacant eyes.

Douglas had always been an imposing figure for Liam. He stood taller than Liam by two inches, his hair black with flecks of gray. He had a well-trimmed beard and was dressed in a tailored suit even on those days when most of the world relaxed in lounge pants, as men were prone to call them, and watched sports.

Presently, Douglas looked like a shell of the person Liam last remembered. He searched his memory for the time of their last meeting. Likely over two years ago—probably more. Distance from his half brother was better for Liam. Being this close in proximity caused a slew of emotions to resurface, and he unconsciously backed away a few steps before he knew what he was doing.

Liam squared his shoulders and walked around the couch so he faced Douglas, and sat down on the coffee table, trying to make eye contact. His brother closed his eyes and leaned his head back.

Douglas's beard was thin and scraggly. He wore flannel pajama bottoms with bear and moose motifs and a worn gray T-shirt. Douglas picked up the glass and took several generous sips. The odor tickled Liam's nose. It wasn't tea. Ashlyn came around from the back of the room so Douglas could see her, but she stayed well enough back—out of lunge range. An animal wary of being present in the room with a predator.

"You're not looking well, brother," Douglas said, leaning forward and gripping Liam's shoulder. "How much you weighing in at these days? One-eighty? Two hundred? Looks like you're not hitting the gym like you used to. Losing muscle mass."

"One-ninety, probably," Liam answered. Everything was always a competition and Liam found it hard not to fall into the trap of one-upmanship. "Want to tell me where your girlfriend might be?"

Douglas picked up the tumbler and aimed his index finger at Ashlyn—a gesture politicians weren't supposed to make. Never point a finger—but Douglas seemed to let the facade slip. "Perhaps you should ask her, since she's the last one that saw Mackenzie." He turned angry eyes toward Liam. "You need to bring my daughter back to me."

One thing Liam knew—he was done being ordered around by his big brother. Seeing Douglas's disheveled state evoked little sympathy in him. "You aren't married to Mackenzie, and we don't know that you are Emory's father. Have to wait for a DNA test on that one. I'm surprised that suddenly you would risk your political career by disclosing an affair—unless you're trying to tug at people's heartstrings by saying your mistress is missing and now you're in charge of raising a small child on your own."

"You assume everything I do is a political calculation."

"You've spent your whole life proving to me it is. Actions are louder than words. Like how kind you were when I came back from overseas."

"What are you talking about?" Douglas asked. "I gave you every opportunity to share your story."

Liam nodded. "That you did. For your gain. You loved nothing more than to call me Operation Death and Destruction."

Liam didn't have to turn around to feel Ashlyn's surprise go through him like a shock wave. Douglas paused and then poured more liquor into his glass. "You were always too sensitive about that."

"Yeah, the death of my best friend raises my ire. Have you adopted the moniker for some reason?" Liam asked.

"Why would I? You seem to own it pretty well all on your own."

Liam measured what his next sentence should

be. Seeing the screen name on the dark web account had increased his suspicion that Douglas was involved in what had happened to Mackenzie, as he had used the term in the past. It was unusual enough to be distinct to their situation and all that was happening, but showing his full hand could be dangerous.

"I had nothing to do with Mackenzie's disappearance," Douglas insisted. "I don't know where she is. And so far, the police haven't taken an ounce of evidence from my home. They can't find anything."

"No surprise to me," Liam countered. "You would never soil the house you live in, to put it nicely."

"You think you know everything about me, but you don't. You don't know how much I care for Mackenzie. You don't know how much I love Emory."

When questioning someone, Liam had been taught to listen closely to the interrogee's words. What tense did they use to refer to people, to their enemies, to know if they might be alive or dead? Douglas referred to Mackenzie in the present tense. Which lent to his theory that she was alive, but where?

"If you care so much for Mackenzie, then you'll remove the contract that you put out on her sister's life."

It was a strategy Liam often used as part of his interrogation techniques. Drop a bomb, preferably something known with evidence to be true, and read the reaction of the prisoner to see what information could be garnered. The idea wasn't necessarily for a confession in return, but to get a read on the body language to see if it was a lie that followed.

Douglas didn't miss a beat. "What contract?"

Not a single tell of deceit. The truth? Or a trained politician in action?

"I'm sure your friend Wesley Taylor informed you. The attack at my cabin. The men at the police station. I'm sure this isn't the first you've heard about those incidents."

"I haven't seen Taylor. First thing I woke up to was a slew of police officers at my door."

"Sleeping pretty late for you. It's early afternoon. You're usually an early riser. Up before dawn. What changed? Guilty conscience keeping you awake at night? Out burying a body?"

It sounded callous, and it was meant to be. Evil men respected a challenge more than polite questioning, in his experience. Liam regretted having to say something so dark in front of Ashlyn, but he was done trying to determine if Douglas was telling the truth.

Still not a slip of betrayal to be noted on his brother's countenance.

"We are going to get married. Why would I want Mackenzie dead?"

"You are *already* married," Liam emphasized.

"I got a divorce. Finalized three months ago."

That was a surprise. Liam had seen nothing reported in the news, but then again—he wasn't in the state of mind to follow asinine local gossip. Douglas stood and headed toward his office. The move made a police officer standing sentry shift on his feet, but he didn't stop him. Douglas extracted two manila envelopes from a safe next to his desk and then placed the red envelope he'd been holding into the safe and locked it. Curious move for a Christmas card. He then pulled the documents from the folders and plopped them on the table with the flair of a king holding his ring out to be kissed by a passing peasant.

Liam knew who he represented to Douglas. What surprised him was how fast Ashlyn crossed the room to grab the papers. It didn't take but a few moments for her eyes to register a realization she was not expecting.

"He's telling the truth," Ashlyn said.

"About which part?" Liam asked.

"All of it," Ashlyn said, her voice a combination of sadness and surprise. Liam wasn't sure he'd ever heard those two tones together.

Liam stepped into the office and eased the papers from her hands. One set was the divorce decree—granted three months prior. And in the other hand, a marriage license for him and Mackenzie. "So Mackenzie took Emily's place? Why couldn't you hold it together for your sons? Give them the stable home that we never had? Love comes and goes. Feelings change over time. Why couldn't you honor the *commitment* you made when you married her?"

"I didn't love Emily anymore. It's as simple as that. I don't have to be beholden to a woman I don't have an emotional connection to for the sake of the children."

Liam tossed the documents back on the desk. "If your feelings change, there is no honoring a commitment? Was there nothing you could do to salvage your marriage? Did you put forth any effort to try?" Liam sniffed hard. "These papers mean nothing. I'm sure your ex-wife was happy to see you go. She and the boys are probably much safer now."

Douglas jammed his thumb into his chest. "I was the one who reported Mackenzie missing."

"Plenty of men who have had a hand in their girlfriend's demise report them missing to throw off the police," Liam said.

The harshness of Liam's words was like a bench press bar on Douglas's shoulders. They visibly pulled down and Douglas reached out to his desk to support his weight with both hands pressed against the walnut surface. He raised his eyes to Liam. "You really think so little of me that your first thought is that I'm behind her disappearance. That I'm responsible for... this dark web contract out on Ashlyn's life and even my baby girl. Whose life I'm trying to save, by the way."

"Funny, I never spoke about the dark web, yet you seem to know something about it." Liam edged closer.

"I'm not talking about a death contract." Douglas walked around the desk and stepped nearly nose to nose with Liam. "I'm talking about finding a cure for Emory's disease."

Liam eased back an inch, not willing to surrender any additional ground. Could this be true? Douglas knew about the disease and was trying to help? He dismissed the thought for now.

"Regarding your probable involvement, I wouldn't believe such a thing if you hadn't shown me how brutal you could be every day of our lives together."

Ashlyn pushed between them, placed a hand on each of their chests and gave a gentle shove, easing them apart. Liam relented, but Douglas remained cemented in his position. Another mark against him in Liam's mind—the inability to stand down in the presence of a woman when tensions were high.

Suddenly, every police radio started squawking. Liam turned, trying to decipher the report coming across.

An explosion in the town.

Mackenzie's house had gone up in flames.


Ashlyn and Liam sat approximately one block away from Mackenzie's splintered home. Night had fallen, and they were waiting for the last of the officers to disappear before trespassing on the crime scene. The last of two cop cars rolled by. Ashlyn was reassured by Liam that they would leave one police officer behind to watch the property until the arson investigation team arrived. It was the only window of opportunity they had, and it would close once the sun came up.

"Ready?" Liam asked.

Ashlyn nodded as she reached for the door and opened it, her body a can of wriggling worms wondering at what they would find and breaking the law. She wasn't sure she'd be able to walk. She leaned over and placed her hands on her knees, taking several deep breaths. She had to do what she could to find out what had happened to Mackenzie, and it was clear they were going to have to do the hard lifting on their own.

She squared her shoulders and stood. "After you."

They were dressed in black. Ashlyn's eyes had long adjusted to the darkness of night. This area of the city was less densely populated, and though the moon was absent, there was little cloud cover, and the stars provided enough light that they didn't need flashlights as they navigated the wooded lot behind Mackenzie's property.

The home was three stories. An odd Victorian structure. Ashlyn pulled up as she took in the devastation. One side of the house had evaporated. In the blast's wake, what remained was splintered and charred wood open like a hungry lion's mouth chewing at the sky. Liam turned back toward her and reached out his hand. She grabbed it and he gently pulled her forward.

First, they walked along the side of the property. There were no lights inside the house. Near the front, Ashlyn could see an officer sitting in his car, the yellow cast from his cell phone illuminating his face. Likely an officer of lower rank pulling in overtime for this duty, considering the other investigations going on in the city. If they could stay near the back of the house and use as little light as possible, they could slip in and out before being noticed.

Liam eased back, and Ashlyn followed. They climbed the steps to the back porch. Ashlyn got down on her hands and knees and looked for the fake stone that held the house key. Not the smartest place to hide a key, but beneficial for them at this moment. It was harder in the dark than she'd imagined, but her fingers coursed over something that felt plastic versus stone and she turned it over and slid open the compartment. The silver key glinted as Liam shone a small light.

She eased it out, stepped up to the door and slid the key into the lock, holding her breath until it turned and the lock released.

The smell of smoke, faint on the outside, was overwhelming once the door opened, and Ashlyn coughed a few times, trying to keep the sound muffled in her chest by pressing her lips together. She slipped the key into her pocket.

Liam aimed the flashlight toward the center of the mudroom. Winter clothing was strewn about the floor, having been knocked off their pegs by the blast. They stepped through puddles of water as they made their way into the kitchen, which was relatively intact. The floorboards creaked as they walked across them. Certain areas of the floor gave way like a soaked sponge. How secure was this structure? When they entered the kitchen, they saw a red envelope in the center of the table.

A crisp red envelope. With Douglas's name written on it. The writing the same as the one on the red envelope back at his house.

Ashlyn reached out to grab it when Liam stopped her. "That rock in the backyard that held the key. Was it in the normal spot?"

"No, but there have been people all over this yard today. It could have been knocked out of place."

"Someone came here after the fire and placed this here for someone to find later. Did Douglas know about the key?"

"I'd assume so, but he has his own key."

Ashlyn didn't want to think about the key and how someone had gained access to the property. She only wanted to see what was in the note. They'd already broken the law. She reached for it again.

Liam pulled her back. "I want to know what it says, too, but this could be the only piece of evidence that leads to your sister. We don't want our fingerprints all over it and screw up others that someone might have left behind."

"We are here breaking the law. I thought we were in this to save our lives. We have people trying to kill us and you're stopping me from looking at the one clue we found?"

Liam pressed a finger to his lips, clearly worried that her rising voice would travel the distance through the cool night air and alert the police officer out front. He whispered, "We don't have access to a police lab."

"Remember who the head of the local police is. You think Wesley Taylor is going to properly analyze this evidence if he's in your brother's pocket?"

Liam raised an eyebrow. Ashlyn reached into her coat pockets, pulled on a pair of leather gloves and then wiggled her fingers in front of Liam, proving she wasn't as reckless as he was making her out to be. He crossed the kitchen and found a paring knife and handed it to her. She eased it in the gap and sliced the envelope open and pulled out the contents.

It was a ransom note asking for money in payment for Mackenzie's life. One million dollars from Douglas. Ashlyn's mind filled with relief.

Mackenzie was alive. All she had to do was pay these people off and Emory could have her mother back. How could she secure that amount? She didn't have it in her bank account. If Douglas was truly innocent, he should be more than willing to pay the money. He had the funds to do so.

Liam took the note from her fingers and read it, not saying what he was thinking.

"She's alive," Ashlyn asserted.

"Ransom notes aren't proof of life."

She ripped the note from his fingers. "She's alive."

In her mind, stating it made it more workable, but she could see the concern in Liam's eyes. She could sense he wanted her prepared for the worst. Medicine functioned that way. Ashlyn didn't want her personal life to be the same.

"We're going to get this money—" she insisted, as if to convince herself.

The floor creaked louder, and Ashlyn was falling. She landed hard, dust and ash kicked up, and she inhaled a lungful of particles. She was on her side when Liam crashed through the floor a few feet away from her.

She could breathe. *Calm down. Calm down. Calm down.* The repeated mantra was an antidote against the adrenaline her body flooded into her veins. She willed herself to take small breaths. Each inhalation brought a series of racking coughs that further made it difficult to breathe. She took stock of her body as she would assess a patient.

*I know who I am. I know where I'm at. I know who Liam is. I don't have any numbness or tingling in my hands or feet.*

She'd landed on a pile of fractured boards and housing debris. Remnants of blankets and clothing. Pieces of Emory's crib. She looked up and saw the gaping hole in the basement ceiling opened by their weight on the weakened joists. Her nerves tingled thinking about the harm that would have come to Emory if the explosion had occurred when she was there.

Ashlyn eased onto her back, able to take slightly deeper breaths. Pain seared through her chest as the air sacs in her lungs hungrily fed on the inhaled oxygen and popped open. Her vision blurred, and she remained still for a few moments until it cleared. She wouldn't be able to check on Liam until she could breathe and move herself.

Another deep breath. Minimal pain. Ashlyn wiggled her toes and fingers. Check. She reached to her head and patted it. The old gunshot wound still felt tender, but it didn't look like she had any new devastating injuries. She felt her neck and tentatively moved it side to side, up and down, and touched her chin to her neck. No pain.

Slowly, she sat up. At first, she couldn't see Liam, the hull of the basement as dark as a cave in the depth of night.

"Liam?" Her voice was not as strong as she needed it to be. There was the sound of footfalls above. The lone officer sitting at the house's front had heard the commotion and decided it warranted further investigation.

"We're down here. We need help!" Ashlyn yelled.

"All right, hang on. Let me get the fire department on the way."

Ashlyn grabbed her phone, turned on the flashlight and scanned the area. Liam had fallen behind her and was facedown with a bunch of splintered boards covering his back. Ashlyn found her footing and made her way to him, gingerly stepping through the debris. Several exposed nails jutted up, hoping to puncture fresh skin.

The fear in her heart spread dread throughout her system. Every step forward without seeing him move fed into her belief that he might be dead. What would she do then? What would she do without him? The thought struck her. She had become wholly dependent on this man like they'd been in a close physical relationship longer than in reality. The depth of their emotional connection was stronger than she wanted to admit.

She knelt next to him, placed her hand on his back and felt the steady rise and fall. That meant his heart was beating. His chest rise was equal, which ruled out a deflated lung. She nudged his shoulder. "Liam, wake up."

He reared up on his knees, furtively looking about. He grabbed a splintered two-by-four, placed it on his shoulder as if holding a weapon and scanned the basement.

Liam was not with her in this reality. She did not know where he was.

# EIGHT

Liam coughed as fine cement particles invaded his lungs. The blast was unexpected and the fall through the floor had left him stunned. The sun was bright overhead, and he scanned the debris for his partner, Brian.

Something was off. The world was wavy… like heat lifting off a highway in the desert. His weapon felt tactically different from the one he'd carried while in the military. Lighter. The trigger wasn't in the right place. He wiped his eyes and brought his hand down.

Blood.

"Brian!"

"Liam, he's not here. You're with me. We fell through the floor at my sister's house." A woman's voice. Furtively, he twisted his body one hundred and eighty degrees to catch sight of her. There was a pressure on his forehead but not by any hand he could see. "You've cut yourself in the fall. Let me help you."

He must be imagining things. Liam reached up and felt a hand, but not the body connected to it. He batted the sensation away, rolling from the hallucination no matter how tempting it was to have that touch stay in contact with him. The physical touch had a calming effect on his elevated heartbeat and the breath coming quick in and out of his chest. Whatever was happening couldn't distract him from finding his partner buried somewhere in the rubble. The mortar had hit the first floor, and the roof had caved—sending them falling through two floors. Liam scanned the beige terrain with the weapon again and, after not seeing any threats, he shouldered it. With two hands, he began moving cinder blocks to find Brian. Again, the rocks did not feel right in his hands. They were lighter than expected and he hastened through the area when he saw the bloodied hand reaching out.

He ran over the pile of rubble and knelt, taking Brian's hand in his, pressing his second and third fingers into the groove of his wrist. There was nothing. No pulse after more than a minute of praying for one. The hand was not as warm as it should be.

"Liam!"

Pressure on his shoulders. The scene grew cloudy...darkness edging into view. The smell of broken lumber and musty, humid air filled his nostrils, replacing the sandiness of the desert. Drops of water landed on his face as he looked up and saw not a single white wisp of cloud cover.

He felt two hands on his face and that was when the desert landscape collapsed, and it plunged his vision into darkness. He blinked rapidly, trying to sort out the puzzle in front of him. Was what he was seeing now a hallucination formed as an escape from the desert and the death of his friend?

Then he saw Ashlyn and those green eyes boring into his, trying to pull his soul back to the present. He dropped the piece of wood and sat on his haunches, grabbing on to both of her hands, doing some things he'd only read about in books about how to manage symptoms of post-traumatic stress, but had never tried. Grounding himself to the here and now. Feeling every moment of the present through all his sensations to bring him back to reality.

Liam took slower breaths, feeling the warm, soft flesh of her hands between his. The faint hint of her, something fruity with an undertone of floral—like oranges and the smell of lavender that his mother tried to grow once—eased the smell of baking sand from his nostrils. Ashlyn pressed closer to him, using the bottom of her shirt to dab against the wound on his forehead to stem its bleeding. He reached one arm around her, pulling her toward him, and settled his head against her chest, feeling the slower nature of her breathing and matching it with his own. A lifeline he could not live without.

His heart rate remained elevated. What would she think? He'd kept so much hidden from her in his letters. He'd never disclosed these dissociative states and what brought them on. Part of the isolated cabin life was to keep triggers like this at bay. He had relived a real-life event—when he'd lost a dear friend in Afghanistan because of a mortar attack that he hadn't seen coming. The rest of that day had been unearthing a body that would only go into the ground again when returned to his home continent and to his family, so they'd have a grave to visit.

The emotions of that day lingered in him like stench. The tightness at the back of his throat. The cries of distress as he radioed for help, hoping that his comrades would get to Brian in time to coax him back into this life from wherever he had gone.

How could there be a loving God when there was death and war? Where humans fought to kill one another over whatever ideal they claimed to be more important than another's life? He could feel the racks of emotion overtaking him, and he held on to Ashlyn with both arms, bringing her closer.

"I'm with you," Ashlyn said.

He was so thankful she hadn't tried to come up with some platitude to ease his suffering, because there were no words she could say that would lessen the overwhelming sadness that enveloped him like a suffocating cloud of smoke.

She raked her hands through his hair. More footfalls from above. The cavalry in the form of the fire department was coming to pull them from the basement. He still somehow had the ransom note clutched in his hand.

How was he going to explain all this to Taylor? He suspected Taylor had a hand in all that was happening and was offering cover for the true criminal that was his brother. Liam opened his eyes and looked up. Above through the gaping hole, two faces with black firefighter hats peeked down.

"Are you two all right?" one yelled down.

Liam found his footing and stood. "We're both relatively uninjured. Able to walk."

"All right, we'll get someone down to you. Give us a few minutes."

Liam looked at Ashlyn, took in every inch of her he could see in the dark, moving his hands over her to look for injuries.

She stilled them. "I'm okay. What happened? You were…somewhere else."

"I was back…in the desert. The sound of the floor breaking and us falling through was very similar to something that happened to me in Afghanistan. A friend of mine…didn't make it. I relived that day all over again…like I was physically there."

Liam turned away from her. He didn't want to see the look in her eyes, regardless of what they held. Forgiveness would mean that he had done something that warranted an apology. Pity meant she would never see him as an equal—he would always need to be looked after. Compassion meant he was broken, and would confirm all he believed about him never being fully able to be the partner she deserved. And that was what he wanted to see the least.

If he was always being pulled back into the past, into these dark memories without warning, then he could never be fully present with her—and she ultimately deserved his full presence. He wouldn't conscript her to a life of service with someone who was fractured and never capable of standing on his two feet.

A rope dropped through the hole and two firefighters propelled down.

"Let's get the two of you out of here. There

are a few law enforcement officers that are eager to ask you questions."

They hoisted Ashlyn up, and at that moment Liam felt comfortable enough to look at her back as they worked to take her back up the hole.

The firefighter who remained reached forward. "You've got a nasty cut there. Going to need stitches."

"Nothing that a few butterfly closures won't fix."

"I think you might be more busted up than you think," the firefighter said.

That was truer than Liam was going to admit.

Ashlyn watched Sheriff Black pace back and forth between them. Liam had reached out to him for help even though Mackenzie's house was in Taylor's jurisdiction, and they were waiting for the police chief's arrival. They'd been separated by a few feet, so they could not talk with one another. Black had the ransom note in his hand after Liam had surrendered it. Liam sat on the end of an ambulance gurney. He'd let them treat the cut by washing it out and closing it with some tape, but he was refusing transport to the hospital.

"What made either of you think this was a good idea? You trespassed onto a crime scene and nearly got yourselves killed. Who knows what evidence you destroyed!"

Ashlyn shuddered. Liam seemed unfazed by the yelling. Of course, he'd lived through much worse than someone screaming. The experience of having mortar shells explode around you probably put Black's raised voice in the range of a whisper to Liam.

"You're going to be charged with trespassing or tampering with evidence," Black said as he saw Chief Wesley Taylor walking their way. "There's no way Taylor is going to let this go. You'll be lucky if he doesn't lock the two of you up until you can see a judge."

"That's not smart," Liam said. "It'll trap us in a place that will be easy to breach. Best thing would be to charge us and give us a court date and see if we can make sense of this ransom note."

Black held the evidence bag up that contained the letter. "You know what this just did? It's going to get the FBI involved because it's kidnapping for ransom. They're likely to take the case over and then none of us will be able to help you."

Wesley Taylor sidled up next to Black. "He's right on all accounts, but you're right, too, Liam."

Ashlyn blinked hard. Hearing Taylor relent to anything Liam said was surprising. It didn't seem to be in his nature to succumb deferentially to an enemy.

"What are you going to do about the note?" Ashlyn asked.

Taylor took the offered note from Black to review. After a few moments, he shrugged. "Black's right. Mackenzie's disappearance is going to be out of our hands. The FBI will get involved."

"How long can you hold them off?" Liam asked.

"I don't know. I'd be delinquent in my duties if we didn't notify them ASAP. The note isn't very specific about a time and place to leave the cash. It's merely a demand and not a lot of follow-through."

"How much time do we have to get out of town? We don't have time to be questioned right now," Ashlyn said.

"You assume I'm letting you leave." Taylor crossed his hands in front of his body. "It's going to take them time to get a plan in place. They'll need to set up monitoring equipment at Douglas's house to record any communications, but someone has been watching this property. My team made a sweep through here after the fire and nothing like this was sitting on the table. It would have been discovered today when Forensics came back. The benefit of leaving it after the fire means that Mackenzie's camera system wasn't up and functioning, so no images of the culprit would be garnered."

"Is there anything you can do to determine who left it?" Ashlyn asked.

"We're checking the surrounding houses to see if they might have any footage. Problem is that the person or persons could have entered the home the same way you did…through the woods in the dead of night, which will make it more difficult to get any clear images."

Liam looked at Taylor. "Douglas has an envelope like this one at his house. Writing on it is the same."

Taylor raised a quizzical eyebrow. "It could also have been a Christmas card you saw."

"Then why would he put it in his safe?" Liam challenged.

"I'll ask him about it. Getting a ransom note doesn't implicate anyone in a crime. In fact, it might prove that what he's saying is true. That he doesn't have anything to do with what's happening in Jackson."

Black and Taylor walked away. Liam stood up to pace off some of his energy. He neared the duo, who seemed to be talking strategy. All were tired, resigned. No arguments ensued.

Ashlyn reached out and grabbed the forearm of the paramedic who had provided first aid to Liam. "How'd the cut look?"

"Needs stitches, but he's refusing. Perhaps you could convince him to be seen. I had little success."

"Liam's lived through much worse. He won't

waste time getting stitches. The more devastating wounds…you can't see them."

"Military, then," the man replied.

"How'd you guess?" Ashlyn asked.

The man pulled a set of dog tags from underneath his shirt. "Your friend…is he having trouble?"

"When we were in the basement, he was seeing something that wasn't there. He said the fall transported him back to when he lost a friend over in Afghanistan."

"It's called a dissociative state. Disconnecting from reality is one of the more severe symptoms of PTSD. I only know this because I've had a few myself. It's like the brain gets short-wired. Memories are not filed away correctly in the mind, so when something happens that closely resembles a traumatic incident, it can pull you back there. I'm no expert, but I've had something like that happen to me. I got treatment."

"What did you do for the military?" Ashlyn asked.

"Not much different from what I'm doing now. I was a medic."

"You saw a lot?"

"All of us see a lot. Even the person not operating on the front lines sees more than your average person."

"You're…healed now?"

The man smiled as she struggled to find the right words. "I don't know if any of us fully heal from the things we see in war. We learn how to manage the symptoms better, so we don't get swept away by them."

"Did you get treatment in this area?"

"There is a doctor that specializes in the type of therapy I received." He reached back for his wallet and pulled out a card. "The treatments are not for everyone, and of course she would need to evaluate him first to see if she thinks he's a suitable candidate. It's like everything in medicine—not every available treatment works for every patient, but if you can convince him to see her, it's at least a starting place."

She pulled the card from his fingers. "Thanks. I appreciate your time and you sharing your experience with me. Thanks so much for serving our country."

"No thanks needed, but I appreciate the words." He grabbed his kit as he gave her a wary smile and then looked past her.

Ashlyn turned around and collided with Liam as she took a step forward. How much had he heard?

"You trying to find a shrink for me?" he asked, his tone edged with accusation. She backed up two steps.

Her words froze in her throat. She didn't want

to say the wrong thing and further push him away, but neither did she want to see him continue to isolate himself if his symptoms could improve. "That man also served in the military. He's had experiences like yours. I asked if he knew anyone who could help."

Liam tightened his lips. "I'm not asking for help. I'm not asking *for you* to find me a therapist. I can manage this on my own."

"Are you, though?" Ashlyn asked. "Managing it? Because all I see is you hiding in fear. Isolating yourself because you can't manage these triggers. Pushing away friends like Doc because you're punishing yourself for things that were never your fault."

Liam tapped his head. "My mind is not working right. What you should do after this is all over is hightail it right on out of here. Go back to your previous life. Forget me. Forget everything. Forget we ever met."

"I won't be able to do that, Liam." She tentatively stepped forward, and he turned his eyes away from her. "Your mind is not broken. It's injured. Like the cut to your forehead. Injuries can be helped. Just like you would go to the doctor for a fracture, there are doctors that specialize in these experiences you're having. They can help you manage the symptoms so you're not living in terror."

"You don't know why I have these feelings."

"Then tell me. Tell me what you think is too dark for me to handle."

"If I did, you'd never come within three feet of me."

Ashlyn reached for his forearm, and he stepped back. "I'm not as frail as you think. I've seen a lot. I've held children in my arms as they died because no family would come to them. I've sung very off-key songs of praise as they took their last breaths. I'm not comparing my work with the viciousness of yours…that I cannot imagine…but I can handle whatever it is you've consigned yourself to this prison for. I know you, Liam. I know you better than you think I do, and I know that you're a good man."

He turned back to her, a different determination in his eye. "This is the plan. We solve whatever happened to Mackenzie—we get you and Emory safe and make sure they take the contracts off the dark web. I'll help you with this, but then I'm not sure there's a compelling reason for us to continue once the mission is complete."

He walked back toward the sheriff and Chief Taylor. Ashlyn buried her face in her hands and tried to dam the tears that coursed down her cheeks.

Would there ever be a chance for them to be together?

# NINE

Liam hated himself for the words he said to Ashlyn. As he headed away from her, his legs felt weighed down—the guilt of his actions lining his feet with lead. Problem was, what he'd said to her was all a lie. He couldn't imagine his life without her and the secret he kept was like poison in the well of their relationship, preventing them from growing closer past this point. If he pushed her too hard, he would have no one else to blame but himself for the estrangement. It would be a self-fulfilling prophecy in every respect of the word.

Maybe that was why Ashlyn felt so comfortable having a close relationship with God. Maybe a better way to live life was to stop leaning on your own self when life was a mess and start leaning on someone else, because he had made little progress moving forward in life trying to manage these issues on his own.

Sheriff Black and Chief Taylor turned toward

him as he neared them. It set a chill through Liam's gut, seeing them in close conversation. Liam had faith in Black, but a halted conversation when someone approached meant secrets, and that made his suspicion of Taylor cast a shadow over Black as well. He was running out of friends that he would willingly trust their lives with. ·

Black nudged his cowboy hat down, so it was harder to look directly into his eyes. That also didn't give Liam any confidence that he was helping him.

"Are you taking us in?" Liam asked.

Both men looked at each other, but remained silent.

"As in, are we under arrest?" Liam pushed. He was exhausted and out of patience. The anger in his voice was a residual effect of his self-loathing for saying things to Ashlyn that he regretted but couldn't keep from spilling over. His usual coping mechanism was to go outside and chop through a few logs for the fire, but that wasn't a viable option at this point.

Furtive glances passed between the sheriff and police chief. Liam fisted his hands. He wanted so desperately to feel like he could depend on someone…anyone. And now the one person besides Ashlyn and Doc he'd confided in was wearing a muzzle. What did Taylor have to do with that? It would seem like the county sheriff would have more power than a local city chief of police.

Taylor turned to Liam. "You've put everyone in a bind, Liam—"

"Me, or the criminals who are wreaking havoc on our city by hunting down innocent people? Do you mean those who are trying to offer cover for criminals because they have political power?"

Taylor seethed. "Are you accusing me of something?"

"I'm just stating the obvious."

"Which is?"

"You've been in my brother's pocket since Douglas snuck cigarettes and liquor from my father's cabinet, and you've been covering up his misdeeds ever since. Are you involved with what's happening here? Did you sneak in and leave that ransom note after your lackeys secured the scene? So Douglas would look innocent?"

Sheriff Black placed his fist in Liam's chest and shoved him back a foot. "You're way out of line, Liam. Even if there's bad blood between the two of you, I'll not stand here and see you accuse someone of crimes without offering proof of your accusations. You'll not smear the reputation of another law enforcement officer in my presence with those conspiracy theories just because your feelings are hurt. Are we clear?"

Liam exhaled sharply. "We're clear. I would suggest you take control over whatever evidence this man and his team uncover to prevent any from coming up missing."

"That's enough, Liam," Black said.

Chief Taylor removed his hat and clutched it between his hands as if to keep them busy enough to think first before smashing one of them into Liam's jaw. "Let's consider the crimes you've committed here. You've crossed a crime scene and contaminated evidence. Normally, I'd take you down and get you booked for that, but considering keeping you in one place could get my station shot up, I will not do that."

"I guess that's *one* thing I can be thankful to you for," Liam said.

"However, I'm going to reserve my option to charge you once we see how things pan out. Next, I'd normally say stay in town, but to be honest, neither I nor the sheriff think that's a good idea. Whatever you're doing to solve this mystery—make sure it doesn't interfere with our work. And it would be best if you left Jackson…for the short term, at least."

Black cleared his throat. "That's generous, Liam. You should grab Ashlyn and get on out of here while the going's good, as they say."

"I guess we're really on our own," Liam said, his voice stiff.

"Considering our number of monthly investigations have quadrupled in the last seventy-two hours, I don't see that any police resources will be available to you, and I'm sure Sheriff Black agrees."

Liam turned to look at Black, who would not meet his eyes. Seemed like the bridge between him and the sheriff was on fire and Liam didn't know if it would stand once the smoke cleared.

At that moment, he saw Ashlyn was about to cross the road and walk to the place they'd stowed their vehicle. She caught his eye and held her hand out to him for the keys.

"Where are you going?" Liam asked.

"I've called Dolores and I'm going to pick up Mackenzie's…things." Seemingly, Ashlyn didn't want to admit to her sister having a journal in front of Black and Taylor for fear of them confiscating the item as evidence. Recent events were pulling her toward her sister's words that had thus far been kept safe. Would Mackenize have written about things she didn't want exposed considering Douglas's nature? Was she suspicious of him?

"We can't go to Doc's. It's not safe for Emory."

Ashlyn motioned Liam away from the group. Once at a safe distance, she said, "I need Mackenzie's journal. It's the only thing we have left that might offer any clues."

Liam reached for his phone and texted Doc with a meeting place. He instructed Doc that Dolores should be escorted by one of his armed buddies.

"Doc's going to make sure she's able to leave the property without being followed. We'll meet in about four hours. Enough time for Doc to co-ordinate and make sure everyone is safe."

Ashlyn turned away from him and headed for the street. It was the roar of the engine Liam heard first. A quick growling acceleration that drove his body into motion. Ashlyn's feet had just touched the pavement when he saw the flash of emerald green in his peripheral vision. She was about twenty steps ahead of him. He prayed he could close the gap before the car did. He bit his tongue to keep from calling her name, as he didn't want to stall her forward progress.

Unfortunately, the sound of the revving engine paused her motion, and she didn't have the few milliseconds for her brain to calculate what was happening and get her body to move out of the way in time.

Liam shoved her hard to the other side of the road, jumped up, contacted the windshield and rolled over the top of the vehicle until he smacked down on his back onto the pavement.

He refused to let the pain stop him from sitting up to catch the license plate. A cacophony of male voices thrummed in his ears as several police officers ran toward them. One officer jumped in his car, but Liam knew it was too late. Whoever had tried to run Ashlyn over likely paid cash for the vehicle, and even if Liam could have made out the license plate and they could run a trace on it, the car would be abandoned somewhere on the side of the road for the police to find nary a clue as to who was involved.

Black ran up to him and placed a hand on his shoulder. "Stay down. Let's get EMS over here to check you out again."

Liam waved him off and made his way over to Ashlyn. She was pulling herself to a sitting position and nursing the abrasions on her palms. She was pale and shaking.

"Can you walk?" Liam asked.

She nodded a response, and he helped her to her feet. Above all else, they needed to rest. Who knew what the day would bring?

Despite Black's protest, he walked Ashlyn to their vehicle and got in. He should stay and give a statement, but there were enough witnesses to give the police that.

For now, they needed a safe place to hide until they met with Dolores. Liam needed to work to build at least one bridge back to Ashlyn.

\* \* \*

A small hunting cabin a few miles outside of town was where Liam took Ashlyn. They'd driven straight there. Liam had suggested to her that a straight shot was a better idea versus a meandering route, giving people less time to spot them again. He'd traded his SUV with one belonging to an officer, hoping to lose the multiple people who were trying to kill them.

Were there really this many evil people in the world? Those that would choose to do harm over a few dollars. Albeit the amount in this case was one hundred thousand dollars. What criminals seemed to risk was being caught and losing the chance to enjoy that money. What made the gamble worth it to them? Or had evil so clouded their vision to such a degree that they couldn't see the hint of truth trying to shine its light through their decisions? One thing Ashlyn knew from nursing was that many people made life so much harder than it needed to be.

She couldn't stop shaking. By now, the adrenaline should have worn off, but she couldn't get warm. The fright of the event chilled her blood, and it bathed each cell of her body. Liam would reach over and try to console her, a reassuring hand on her knee. All she could do was huddle against the door.

They entered the cabin. Liam motioned her to

sit on the threadbare couch. He rifled through the cabinets until he found some hot chocolate and filled the kettle on the stove with water. In the small bedroom he found a pile of blankets and covered her up, rubbing her shoulders to ease her shaking. After finding a box of matchsticks, he made quick work of starting a fire in the rusted woodstove. Ashlyn could barely follow his movements. A heaviness settled over her. A combination of fatigue and overwhelming worry over her loved ones. Could Mackenzie still be alive? Could Doc keep Emory safe? Would Liam stay with her long enough to solve this crime?

Did she want him to?

A single tear slid down her face and she did not have the energy to wipe it away.

The kettle whistled and she could feel the fingers of heat inching into her muscles. She snuggled into the corner of the couch and put her feet up, resting her head on the corner. Liam approached her with a cup of steaming liquid, and she reached for it, wrapping her hands around it as another source of heat, inhaling the peppermint chocolate scent and steam.

"I'm sure it's not as good as your chai, but it should take the chill away."

Ashlyn wanted to speak but couldn't bring herself to. To say her emotions were tumultuous was an understatement. It was more like they were in a bomb cyclone, and just as she was about to sort through what she was feeling, they would get torn up and tossed aside again. Ultimately, she wanted to thank Liam for saving her life…again, but the anger she felt at his words kept her from feeling grateful. How could they ever move forward? Should they move forward? Was it better for Ashlyn to separate from Liam and work with a law enforcement agency like the FBI? Even though it would likely be slower, there wouldn't be the emotional wave she'd been riding ever since she left Emory on Liam's doorstep.

A light snow fell outside. Ashlyn didn't risk sipping the fluid yet. The abrasions on her hands stung, and she needed to get them washed and bandaged. Last thing she needed to deal with was infection setting in a few days from now. Same for Liam's cut—she had to figure out a way to get it stitched.

Liam stood at the end of the couch, and Ashlyn pulled her legs up so he could sit.

For several minutes, they both sat there looking anywhere but at each other.

"I'm sorry…" Liam started. "I didn't mean to lash out at you."

"You didn't mean what you said? Or you're sorry that you hurt me?"

Liam clutched her shin. "Definitely the latter. I'm not sure about the former."

Ashlyn nodded her head. Inside, her stomach tilted and there would not be a way she could keep down the hot chocolate.

Liam rubbed his forehead. "I shared a lot with you in my letters. The things I was most comfortable with, but I kept a lot of things closed off—even though confessing them on paper would have been easier than saying this to you in person."

Ashlyn stilled. She couldn't tell from the look on his face what information was coming. Both hope and dread coupled in her heart, leaving it beating fiercely behind her ribs.

"They had given us a mission to hunt down a serial bomber. The guy was crafty. He'd taken out several of our men and we were eager to get the carnage to stop. We all wanted to feel... safer. Seems like such a strange word, considering the territory we were in. But feeling even a little more at ease could mean getting a good night's sleep."

Ashlyn gripped the mug in her hands, hoping the warmth would stave off the heartrending terror of his words. She'd begged him to share this. Could she handle it?

"There was intel about a hovel he was operating out of, and we went there to see if we could flush him out. As part of SEAL training, I have some limited knowledge of how to defuse bombs, and a lot of the other guys who were more expert had already been dispatched out for the day and weren't available. I guess I know enough to be dangerous, as they say."

Liam smoothed his hands over his face and swallowed hard. Ashlyn's ears tingled with dread at his words. It was easy to claim she supported him when the distance between them meant safety from having to deal with the hard subjects.

"We entered the property and immediately knew we were in the right location. I mean, it was a treasure trove of information and would likely lead to the capture of other bad guys— heads of terrorist groups that were disrupting normal life for everyday citizens. While some of us were looking and gathering up the records as quickly as we could—it was never a good idea to stay in the same place for too long with a US flag patched to your chest—another soldier accidentally hit a trip wire. We were lucky in the sense that it didn't go off right away and kill everyone."

Liam clutched his knees with his hands, pulling his shoulders up near his ears. He made several false starts to continue the story—but was unable to. Ashlyn could see he was struggling with holding back tears. His eyes glazed, and his jaw was set firm. He put his hands to the side of his head and rocked himself for a good minute before he felt the strength to carry on.

Ashlyn didn't know if she could bear to hear these words, but she also knew that holding this space with Liam was the one thing that God wanted her to do. God didn't turn away from His people when they were suffering. And if she believed in the things she said she did, she couldn't turn away from this story. She wanted to sit up and lean forward, offer him an ounce of physical comfort, but she feared any movement would carry her feet right out the door. She'd witnessed enough death in her private life and at work and didn't know how prepared her mind was to accept these things. What would she do with this information? Would it change how she felt about Liam?

"We followed the trip line to the source. There were two young children sitting back-to-back—tied to chairs. The bomb in between them. I raced forward, not thinking clearly, to evacuate them from the structure when another soldier pointed out that you couldn't free the children from the chairs without detonating the bomb and there was a timer counting down… with little time remaining."

Ashlyn closed her eyes. Not to imagine it, but

to shut off forthcoming images. Despite her efforts, such a scene played out in her mind. The broken cement of the structure this man operated out of. The fine particles of dust in the air that choked like the heaviest humidity, only not a drop of water in sight. The peril of those two children and knowing that if Liam suffered as he did with this scenario, then the outcome had not been a positive one.

Liam's voice broke. "They sent the wrong man that day. I took a quick look at the bomb and knew I didn't have the knowledge to disarm it. If I tried, my entire team would die. I...tried to stay to do what I could...not caring for my own life. I asked...begged the others to leave me behind because dying myself would have been easier to live with than the burden I do now. My team literally picked me up and dragged me out to save my life."

He didn't need to continue. What had happened that day to those children was obvious. Ashlyn knew she had to say something, but also knew that she would likely say all the wrong things.

"I'm sorry that happened to you. You should have never been put in that position. No one should ever have to face down evil like you did that day. I wish you had shared this with me sooner."

Liam looked at her…unbelievingly. "You do?"

Ashlyn put her legs on the ground and set the mug on the floor. She reached for him, eased his head onto her lap and began to rake her fingers through his hair as he cried. He gripped her legs between his arms.

Platitudes never offered comfort in these situations. She'd heard them herself when a child died on her watch, and though she could intellectualize that it was the disease process and not her hand that caused the demise, the question she always asked herself was, why did God put her there if not to heal? Why had He put Liam there if not to save those children? Was it just to witness suffering? How did God help when humanity cried out? What people needed was God with a flaming sword coming down from the heavens to serve justice.

Often what He gave was silence and darkened skies.

And in that darkness, what remained was only her ability to reach out. To offer comfort to a man that she was falling in love with and didn't want to live without. Without whom she couldn't imagine a life.

"I want to be with you, Liam. If you'll have me. If you'll let me in."

There was a knock at the door, and Ashlyn instinctively froze. Dolores had arrived early.

Liam wiped his eyes, sat up and drew a gun from underneath his shirt. He walked to the door, looked through the peekaboo window and quickly holstered the weapon to let the two people inside.

Liam ushered in Dolores and her escort and bolted the door behind them. "You two run into any trouble?"

Dolores shook her head. "Not a soul in sight."

Ashlyn threw the covers aside and stood. The world tilted and she placed her hand on the edge of the couch. Living off adrenaline and little food over the last couple of days was having negative effects on her body. Dolores seemed to know the state she'd find them in and handed Liam a grocery sack filled with homemade goods. Liam pulled out a container of broccoli cheese soup and homemade bread. "Thanks, Dolores. You're the best cook in Jackson Hole. Don't know if there will be enough here for Ashlyn."

"How's Emory?" Ashlyn asked.

"She's safe and trying to pull out Doc's beard every time he holds her, so that's keeping him on his toes. Taking care of her has honestly been the best thing for us."

Dolores handed the journal to Ashlyn, but when she did, she flipped open the front cover so Ashlyn could also see that her letter to Liam was tucked inside. Dolores leaned forward and whispered in her ear. "Thought you might want to have this, too."

Ashlyn nodded and quickly closed it. That was when Dolores saw the wounds on her hands.

"Those look terrible."

"I know. As soon as you leave, I'll take care of them. And I'll figure out a way to handle Liam's cut."

The escort pulled Dolores back to the door. "Let's get back to the fortress. Don't want to leave Doc alone with Hudson too long. He'll die of boredom listening to that guy's stories."

"You two take care and we'll see you soon," Dolores said.

Not a question, but a statement of fact. If only Ashlyn felt those words would come to fruition. Right now, she felt as if she and Liam were on an ice floe in the middle of choppy ocean waters.

No rescue in sight.

# TEN

Two days after Christmas. Night had fallen. The peace of the season continued to elude them. Liam helped Ashlyn soak her hands in a bin of soapy, warm water. He worked as gently as he could to coax the gravel chunks from her skin. They found some expired triple antibiotic ointment and gauze for a dressing. Expired wasn't great, but better than the alternative. Ashlyn was quiet, contemplative. She'd been reading through her sister's journal, and something brewed behind her eyes. She'd wince now and then, and he'd apologize for hurting her.

"Sometimes pain is necessary in order to bring about healing," she said after one such instance.

"You believe that's true?" Liam asked.

"Of course. In medicine, when we set bones in the right place, there's always a level of agony that comes with it. Healing isn't a pain-free sport."

It was true, of course. Rubbing the tender

flesh of Ashlyn's hands, trying to remove the contaminated soil that could cause a life-threatening infection, was proof of that. What if he could accept that the mind was no different?

He pulled her hands out of the water, took a towel and patted them dry. He eased her hands to his chest and nestled his cheek against hers. He wanted to be closer to her but didn't dare hope for anything more. There was a cataclysm within himself about what he wanted and what he needed. What he wanted was for Ashlyn to always be with him. What he needed was for her to be safe, and he wasn't convinced those two ideals could ever coexist. It wasn't fair of him to tempt her with physical contact if he wasn't sure he could carry through with the emotional fortitude she would need in a mate...in a husband.

The word startled him, and he forced the fantasy from his mind. He pulled back from her and unwrapped the towel from her hands. Grabbing the ointment, he smeared a generous portion over the wounds and wrapped them with the gauze.

"All fixed, for now."

"But you won't let me do anything about the cut on your head?" Ashlyn asked.

"I've had much worse than this and my body laughs off any germ invasion."

"We'll see," Ashlyn countered and headed back to the couch. "I need to show you something in my sister's journal. I'm not sure how I feel about it."

They both sat on the couch, and Ashlyn pulled the journal toward her. "Mackenzie received a letter from a woman by the name of Claire Brown, who lives in Colorado, a few months ago. The address is here, but she makes no mention of them meeting."

"Is the name familiar to you?"

"Not at all. This woman, Claire, says she got Mackenzie's information from one of those genetic websites where you upload your DNA profile to find members of your family…like if you were adopted and know nothing about your biological family."

"What claim did Claire make in the letter?"

"That she's Mackenzie's sister. That when she was a young child, my mother gave her up for adoption."

"Which also means—"

"That I have a sister I never knew about. Look, I think this is a photo of the two of them." She pulled the photo from where it was tucked between pages.

Liam took it. Two children maybe around the age of five. They were dressed in the same green plaid rompers.

"They're twins?" Liam asked.

"What?" Ashlyn responded.

"They're dressed in the same clothing. Maybe your mother tried adopting both of them out but only found a home for Claire and the two of you ended up in foster care. How much older is Mackenzie than you?"

"Two years."

"Why aren't you in the photo?"

"I don't think it's too troubling. Lots of families will just take photos of…twins. I guess if that's what we're saying they are."

Ashlyn returned to reading the journal and Liam remained quiet. What could anyone say when such a life-altering revelation was made?

"Mackenzie doesn't write much about Claire in these entries. Just that the correspondence she was having with this woman wasn't going as she hoped. That Claire was making some unreasonable demands."

"She doesn't say what they were?"

Ashlyn shook her head. "No, but from the entries, Mackenzie fretted about the interactions. She writes she wished she had never submitted her DNA profile to the site."

"Why wouldn't she write about what Claire was demanding?" Liam asked.

"Probably worried that Douglas would eavesdrop or find out."

"Why would she worry about that? Don't you

think if she loved Douglas, she would reach out to him for help?"

"I don't know much about their relationship," Ashlyn said. "About how good or bad it is. You don't seem to, either."

"What if Claire wants something that Mackenzie doesn't want to give up and that's what's making her nervous."

"Like what?" Ashlyn asked.

"The cure for Emory's disease. Douglas mentioned he was working on something. I can't imagine there would be a lot of medication developed for a disease that affects so few. Maybe just one dose or course of treatment. You said it was genetic."

"That's assuming a lot. That Claire has a child. That the child has the illness. That there is a viable cure. We don't know if any of those things are true."

"That's the problem with everything being public—like these DNA databases. You don't know what kind of danger you're tempting to come into your life. Some people have nefarious intentions in mind. This is our next best lead for investigation. To go to Colorado and see what Claire is all about."

Ashlyn nodded in agreement.

"Let's sleep here tonight. We both could use

a good night's rest. I'll plot a course out to this address, and we'll hit the road in the morning."

"You're not worried that staying here will allow someone to find us?"

"Of course I'm worried about it. I also know the stress of not sleeping for days makes it hard to form reasoned decisions. A rattled brain fuzzes thinking, and we need to have our minds as sharp as they can be."

Liam made a pallet next to the couch, found a few dusty throw pillows in the closet and settled on the floor next to Ashlyn. Night came quickly in the winter, and though it would probably have been wiser to travel in the dark, Liam hung on to his conviction.

*Lord, if You can give us anything right now, give us sleep and the ability to think clearly. Keep Ashlyn safe and help us find the evil men so we can get on with our lives.*

Praying felt strange…like speaking in a foreign tongue. Peculiar, but oddly comforting. If that was an ounce of what Ashlyn felt, maybe he should make it more of a practice.

"Do you remember anything from your youth about another sister?"

"I've been searching through my memories, looking for any hint of her, and I honestly cannot remember. Mackenzie would likely have a better recollection."

Ashlyn shifted on her side and closed her eyes. He reached up and smoothed the hair away from her face but kept caressing her skin when there was no simple reason to keep doing so. She reached her hand up and clasped his until her hand slipped away as she fell to sleep.

If Liam could guarantee that this was how their moments would always be…there wasn't a way he would give her up. Unfortunately, moments of peace were far and few between, and the next crisis was just around the corner.

As they loaded their sparse belongings into Liam's newly purchased old truck, Ashlyn could see he was on edge. Liam had been up before dawn, going through their supplies. He didn't want to make many stops. Only those out of necessity. Their drive would take seven hours. Their destination was a northern Colorado town called Fort Collins.

He'd been cleaning his weapons and checking the amount of ammunition they had on hand. It was as if they were going to see not a long-lost relative but the head of a terrorist organization, and Liam's preparations pushed Ashlyn's mind into a state of hypervigilance.

She was used to that space as a nurse, watching for any sign in her patient that they were slipping from this dimension into the next, but she rarely had the accompanying anxiety paired with it.

*This is what Liam must feel all the time. That no place, no situation, no person can be fully trusted, no matter the history you have with them. Lord, please grant us safety on this journey. Keep Liam's mind here in the present with me and help me better understand the trauma that he is going through.*

Liam settled in the driver's seat and gave her a weary smile. "We can make it a few hours before we need to stop and get gas. It will probably be better if we get out of Jackson as fast as we can."

He'd woken her up an hour before daybreak and now the sun was just peeking over the horizon—like how Emory loved it when Ashlyn played the game with her. As they got ready, he'd given her a lesson on how to reload the weapons they were carrying. In case something happened, he wanted her to be able to help him…or herself if he couldn't anymore. The thought distressed Ashlyn, but in nursing, the worst-case scenario was always prepped for. She couldn't be upset with Liam for having the same mindset. Ashlyn rested her head against the window, and it wasn't long before the hum of the wheels against the blacktop lulled her back to sleep.

She didn't know how much time had passed when she felt Liam grip her thigh. "Trouble."

Ashlyn sat straight up and rubbed her eyes. Liam motioned to the rearview mirror, and she turned in her seat to see the black SUV narrowing the distance between them.

"He caught sight of us a few klicks back at the intersection of this road and an old county road—spun around and followed." Liam reached down and eased his six-shot revolver from his ankle and handed it to her. "The way they're coming up on our tail, they don't have good intentions in mind." He turned briefly and slid open the window at the rear of the truck. "You need to slow them down."

"Liam, I've never shot a gun before in my life."

"You have. Once. You were a pretty good shot."

"That was a fluke. No amount of skill involved."

"Ashlyn, this will not end well if we don't get on the offensive. We're out in the middle of nowhere." Liam pulled his phone up to his face. "I don't have a signal on my cell. We're in this valley and I don't know how long it is. Even if we can reach law enforcement, there is no guarantee an officer will make it to us in time."

Liam drew his SIG Sauer from his side holster. Ashlyn unclicked her seat belt and turned around. The black SUV narrowed the gap. Ashlyn's hands trembled so badly she had to rest the barrel on the back of the seat to steady it—a poor sniper's bipod.

Faster than she thought possible, the SUV punched forward and rammed their bumper. The jolt knocked Ashlyn from the seat, landing her in the well on the passenger side like every kid's worst nightmare from school days. She was pinned. Liam swerved into the oncoming lane, slammed on the brake, and the vehicle spun one hundred and eighty degrees. The smell of burned asphalt and rubber from the road skid the tires left behind was heavy.

Ashlyn tried to set her hands down on the floorboards to get her rear high enough to get back on the seat. Liam leaned over to help push her legs to the side so she could right herself. Just as he leaned down, a bullet punched through the windshield and wind whistled through the cab. The high-pitched noise caused Ashlyn's ears to ring.

She plopped back on the seat and looked behind. The SUV had lost distance but had turned and was back on the road, quickly closing the void. Ashlyn squared her shoulders. Liam was right—they were sitting ducks out here. If she didn't help, they would both die, and who knew what would become of Emory.

Ashlyn turned to the back and widened her knees, the stance giving her more balance as the truck jostled from side to side. Liam set a box of bullets between them and then placed one hand on the steering wheel and another on his weapon.

"Maybe I should drive, and you can shoot," Ashlyn said. "You'll have better aim than me."

"I'm a better tactical driver than you. I don't want you to kill them—if you can do anything to slow the vehicle down, that's all I'm hoping for."

Ashlyn didn't see a way she could take out a tire and disable the vehicle. The closer the SUV got, the widest target would be the windshield. It roared close again.

"I'm going to get us back to the edge of the forest I saw a few miles back. At least we can get cover until we make a different plan, but you need to slow them down."

After seeing the effects of motor vehicle accidents, she didn't want to be unsecured from a seat belt if they were in an accident, and the likelihood of that happening was high. She steeled her stance and used one hand on the side of the window to brace herself from the vehicle's movements. The SUV exploded closer, and the widest target loomed in her vision.

She could see two shadowy figures. The windshield tint made it too hard to make out any discerning features. Would the anonymity make it easier on her psyche if she killed one of these men?

Ashlyn aimed and unloaded the chamber into the windshield. She hit it one time and, in that instant, the driver veered left, their tires hitting the rumble strip. The momentum pulled the vehicle onto the dusty shoulder, and it slowed their speed significantly. Liam pumped his fist into the air and let out a hurrah. He clasped his hand on her shoulder and squeezed hard. "We'll need to improve your average some. We're low on ammunition."

A wash of relief soothed Ashlyn's nerves. She popped open the chamber as Liam had shown her and reloaded bullets—several slipping onto the floorboards from her fingers drenched in sweaty fear.

"It's okay. Take a few deep breaths."

She couldn't. This whole thing was a folly. How could they outrun them forever? The SUV was closing up on them again. She wished they hadn't chosen to go with an old clunker of a truck to make it to Colorado, but Liam had insisted that an older model couldn't be tracked electronically and left the other vehicle for the officer to pick up. Now what Ashlyn wanted more was power over stealth. They needed to outrun people, and they couldn't do it in this vehicle.

Up ahead, she could see the grove of trees that Liam had spoken of. The pines were frosted with the frozen dew of the early morning. The aspens were bare—like sickly skeletons reaching toward the sun for warmth. She huddled in her coat. They were dressed for the weather, but not enough for an extended stay out in the cold. Particularly overnight.

The distance closed, and Ashlyn readied her weapon. However, instead of trying to bump them from the rear as they had previously done, the perps swerved to the side and came up next to the driver's-side window.

"Get down and buckle your seat belt," Liam commanded.

Ashlyn did as instructed. Once the belt latched, she tightened it over her lap. They were side by side. Liam unloaded several rounds into the side of the car—punching through the passenger window. The car eased back for a few seconds. Liam handed the gun to Ashlyn for a reload. She leaned forward to get a new clip from the glove compartment. In that instance, the SUV broadsided them, pushing their car into the guardrail. Metal screamed against metal, and Ashlyn's stomach flipped. Liam wiped the icy dread from his forehead. He didn't ask for the weapon back. His eyes skirted their surroundings, looking for an out.

Being pinned against the SUV and the guardrail slowed their speed. Ashlyn lunged forward and grabbed a clip from the glove compartment, released the empty one and slammed the new one in place. Liam rolled his window down, anticipating her move, and leaned forward. She turned and emptied the clip into the side of the car—the wind whipping her hair. When she heard the weapon click dry, she turned forward. With two empty clips, she'd have to work to get the bullets back in. The SUV had eased back, the side of their vehicle littered with gaping holes.

"Anger improves your aim dramatically."

Ashlyn ignored the comment and worked to load the empty clips. She filled one and put it into place as the vehicle pulled up next to them again. Before she could get in position, they rammed the truck from the side, and this time there wasn't a guardrail to keep them on the road. Ashlyn felt the vibration of the tire hitting the rumble strip; then kicked-up dirty snow and debris filled her vision.

They hit a patch of ice that sent them off the road, and the truck pitched, rolling over down a slope through the wooden bodies of naked deciduous trees.

Ashlyn clenched her eyes closed and gritted her teeth. Glass shattered. Shards bit into the exposed areas of her face and hands, reminiscent of fire ants stinging. She pulled her head down close to her legs, thinking a condensed body would be harder to injure. The metal doors caved inward. The roof punched in. When the truck stopped rolling, they were both hanging upside down.

Ashlyn released the seat belt and tumbled to the roof of the truck. She turned over onto her back. She couldn't see any obvious injury to Liam, but there was blood dripping from his head.

She brushed her face to wipe off the dirt and glass. She reached up and placed her fingers at his neck. His pulse was strong, his breathing steady. "Liam!"

He squinted his eyes in response. Ashlyn grabbed a foot and shook it.

"Liam, wake up!"

He opened his eyes and blinked at her.

"What happened?"

Ashlyn immediately worried. Concussion? A more traumatic brain injury than that?

"They ran us off the road. Come on—we need to get out of this truck. They'll come for us if they're alive."

"You're right. They'll do that after you've hit an IED."

Liam had left her again. He was overseas—back in the desert.

Liam could not understand why his breath misted when it was one-hundred-plus degrees outside. He was upside down, the beige top of their Humvee bent inward. He reached toward his head, and when he withdrew his fingers, a thick red fluid draped them. Seemingly, his previous cut had popped open.

*Should have gotten that thing stitched when I had the chance.*

He looked to his left. Brian knelt on the roof, reaching out to him. They couldn't stay in one position long. As soon as the enemy knew they were stationary, their weapon-wielding figures would dot the horizon, and this vehicle and the surrounding area would be a kill zone.

He unclipped his seat belt and fell sloppily onto the roof. His vision phased in and out. He blinked rapidly, his heartbeat racing.

There was snow falling in the desert. He reached to his chest to radio for help and give their coordinates, but underneath his fingertips he felt the coarse fabric of a winter coat and not the nylon texture of his Kevlar vest. He patted for his weapon and found it. Brian held a small gun as well—not military-issue, which further confused Liam.

"Liam, you're with me. Be here with me."

Of course he was here…with Brian. He motioned his finger across his throat and pressed his index finger to his lips, listening to the silence of the sunbaked sand. He heard crunching—not like footsteps over dirt, but like feet crushing crystals. He shook his head to clear his discordant senses. He couldn't make sense of these distinct sensations. Could be that he suf-

fered some nerve damage in the explosion that
was wreaking havoc on his perceptions.

The passenger window behind Brian was
blown out. He pointed out the direction and
shoved Brian through it. Brian turned back to
Liam, waving his hands in front of his face.

"Liam, come back to me."

Liam scurried out of the truck. The sounds of
the first gunshot splintered a tree a few yards
ahead. Liam pushed Brian to the ground. Instead of Brian's face landing on heated earth,
his cheek was encased in a mound of white. His
breath misted as he exhaled. He and Brian lay
face-to-face in snow.

Brian reached out a hand and laid it against
his cheek.

"Liam, you're with me."

Liam's world faded again, and Ashlyn filled
his vision. Remnants of grass and dirt littered
her hair. He inhaled deeply. His nose tingled
with the bite of frost. He reached his hand into
the snow and icy crystals replaced the granules.

Ashlyn pressed her lips against his. He knew
what it was. A desperate attempt to call him back
from the desert into the snow-laden forest. Another
gunshot rang out, and he pulled away from her.

"I'm here—I'm with you." He pulled up on his
elbows and scanned the area. There was a tighter
cluster of trees not far ahead, and he pointed.

"You go first. I'll provide cover. When you get there, get yourself hidden and shoot above my head, and I'll crawl the rest of the way."

Hopefully, Ashlyn wouldn't accidentally shoot him. Having an inexperienced gunman lay down suppressing fire was a risk, but undoubtedly the people following them would not stop after seeing their vehicle fall down the embankment.

Ashlyn nodded and scurried forward. Liam turned around, the truck a crumpled mass of twisted, rusted metal. The scrap yard wouldn't have done as much damage. He could see two figures making their way down the embankment—slipping down the moist grass but following the path their rolled vehicle had taken. One pointed, seeing the crash site, and they picked up their pace. They carried handguns, which was a relief to Liam. They could not fire at them relentlessly with automatic weapons. They wore masks and dark clothing with Kevlar vests. Disabling them might not be as easy as Liam hoped.

He glanced behind. Ashlyn had made it half the distance. Settling on his chest, Liam held the weapon in both hands with his elbows braced against the ground. He'd have to either take a chance with a lethal head shot or wound them enough that continuing this chase, even for the hundred thousand dollars, would be less desirable than keeping their own lives.

Liam zeroed in on the lead male—a stocky guy who ambled down the slope like a linebacker walking up to a scrimmage line. Liam decided a direct hit to the vest was the best option. Likely not deadly but could incapacitate him long enough for Liam to move into the protection of the trees. He was loath to take a life even under these circumstances.

He estimated the yards between him and this stranger, waited until the man took an additional twenty steps, and then fired.

The sound of the gunshot was deafening to his ears. He hit the man—directly in the chest. The man was knocked onto his back and slid down the snow to the base of the hill. The other guy hit the ground and shimmied to his friend. Liam turned and rifled through the truck's corpse to pick up additional ammo. That was when Ashlyn fired indiscriminately above his head. Liam slipped away again...into the desert. He shoved his face into the snow to keep the heat at bay and got up on all fours and crawled toward Ashlyn. As he pulled her into the trees, another round of gunfire broke out, but encased in this womb of aspen branches, Liam felt assured and protected for the moment.

"What's the plan?" Ashlyn asked.

Liam wiped the moisture from his face and handed her a box of ammo. "You're going to keep firing in their direction. I'm going to flank them and try to take them out from the side."

Ashlyn nodded, though he could see the trepidation in her eyes. She'd done so much for him. Hadn't abandoned him when he felt his mind unmoored from the earth. Continued to feel safe in his presence. Could he live through the pain of dealing with his trauma to feel safer around her? What if he'd mistaken her for the enemy instead of a friend? He shook the thoughts away, too terrified to consider what would have happened in the alternative.

He exited the grove from the rear and took a wide arc. He could see the one gunman still on the ground—not moving. Maybe the shot had done more damage than just hitting him in the chest and knocking the wind out of him. Maybe the fall had caused injuries that Liam couldn't see. His partner was attempting to rouse him, but none of the motions was bringing his friend back.

Liam continued running in the wide arc. Ashlyn fired toward the gunmen. The remaining man stood, and just as he did, he took a shot into the shoulder. Liam saw the spray of blood mist red into the snowbank. The man gripped the wound and fell to his knees. He threw the weapon aside and raised his hands in the air—one higher than the other.

Surrender.

Liam closed the distance quickly. Once he was about a hundred yards away, the man reached for his partner's gun and took aim at Liam. Before he could fire off a round, Liam discharged his weapon and hit him in the hand. A scream shredded the silence and the assailant dropped the gun. Liam closed the distance, saw red drops of blood littering the snow. He kicked the weapon away and held the man at gunpoint.

"Get your hands behind your back."

The man whimpered as he moved his injured hand and arm behind. Liam zeroed his gaze on the friend and noticed the subtle rise and fall of his chest. Whatever injury had occurred—he was still breathing.

Liam patted the man down and didn't find any additional weapons. He found a satellite phone and called 911.

"What's your emergency?"

"Two gunmen have run us off the road. I've got them detained, but we'll need rescue and the local sheriff."

Once he gave the best location he could, he grabbed the two weapons and secured them on his body. He lifted the mask off the conscious man and took a step back, the shock causing him to create more distance between him and his enemy.

An enemy he'd once called a friend.

# ELEVEN

Parker Young. They'd been friends. Close friends. They'd gone through SEALs training together, but Parker hadn't made the cut. Rang the bell, signaling his exit. Was Liam living his life much differently from the real-life moment he was remembering? Succumbing to the physical destruction and mental devastation. It was usually the latter that caused people to drop out of SEALs—maybe out of life. In times of difficulty, it was mental toughness that led people to prevail.

*I had it once—that strength of character to push through so much evil. Where did it go? Will I ever feel that way again?*

A follow-up prayer to those thoughts tickled the tip of his tongue. His heart pleaded with his mind to whisper the name of God as a plea for intervention. Liam was coming to the end of himself. The two primary defense strategies that normally worked for him, isolation and detachment, didn't feel effective anymore.

Ashlyn brushed the dirt off her pants as she made her way toward him. She still wore the white winter coat she had on when they'd first met. It was now dotted with the debris of their misadventures—blood, bits of broken pine cones, green stains and cuts through the fabric from shards of glass.

Liam turned his attention back to Parker. He put his foot into his chest to keep him pinned to the ground, the other man still unconscious but breathing.

"Did Douglas put you up to this?"

Parker shook his head. Liam didn't believe it.

"I swear," Parker said, after taking a deep breath.

Liam eased his foot up. "This is what you're doing with your time? Going around the dark web and looking for contracts you can cash in on? This is the choice you make after taking an oath to serve your country?"

"A country that gave up on me," Parker spit.

"Because you didn't get everything you wanted?"

The man turned his eyes away. Liam could hear sirens in the distance. A squad car came to a screeching halt on the embankment. An officer disembarked. Liam holstered his weapon, raised his hands and motioned for Ashlyn to do the same. He backed away from the men on the ground.

The officer drew his weapon, pointing it at each person, trying to find out what had happened.

"These two ran us off the road and then tried to hunt us down," Liam said.

"Then why are the two of them on the ground?" The officer knelt and sank two fingers into the unconscious man's neck to check his pulse, and he kept his gun trained on Liam. He then pulled on a pair of latex gloves and groped around his head, and Liam saw a sheen of blood when he withdrew his hand.

Liam pointed. "That's our vehicle rolled over a few yards back. We ran into those trees for protection and returned fire when they came after us. Let's just say that good prevailed in this situation."

Parker snickered. Two other law enforcement officers arrived. They must be closer to a town than Liam had thought, considering their quick arrival. It would behoove them to stop for the night.

"You can verify my statements by calling Sheriff Tom Black or Jackson police chief Wesley Taylor."

That raised the officer's eyebrows.

The newly arrived officers patted Liam and

Ashlyn down and confiscated their weapons, then separated the two of them. After verifying their stories were similar and the other two men remained mum on the subject, they gave Liam and Ashlyn permission to go back to their overturned vehicle and gather any belongings they needed.

"What are we going to do about the weapons?" Ashlyn asked.

"They should give them back once they clear things here. Let's just get what we need. We'll have to figure out a way to get a ride into town."

Ashlyn sat on the grass and leaned against the bent-up truck carcass. He knew the feeling. The life they were living was overwhelming. Too much danger. Little downtime to process and rest. It was hard to think through all that had happened when thoughts came like a tsunami. Liam noticed the slight tremor in her fingers. She rubbed her hands together, needing the friction to generate warmth. He sat down on the ground, faced her and placed his rough hand on her cheek. She nestled into it, and he pulled her into a hug.

How much more could they take? It was eye-opening to Liam that there had been this much attention given to this contract. It seemed like more than a handful of people were willing to risk the consequences that ranged from death to incarceration for a quick payoff. He'd lived his whole life trying to help others—even if he'd failed at it on some level. For others, they weren't thinking twice about the possibility of getting caught. Just the high from drawing a quick paycheck, no matter how they'd gotten it.

In the middle of all this chaos was Ashlyn. She stayed with him for likely what she considered selfish reasons, but Liam knew she could easily find someone else to protect her. She could work with law enforcement, but maybe she too had been disillusioned by seeing how cozy the police and politics were when it came to Douglas and the chief. That sometimes, the two were so intertwined they couldn't think as individuals anymore.

Liam thought back through the events they'd survived. How many more crises would there be like this? How many more times could they escape the reaper's scythe?

There was one thing Liam needed to correct. Their first kiss. If such a thing could be done. He didn't want Ashlyn to remember it as a tactic she had used to save him from himself. He wanted her to know that their first kiss would have all the intention of his feelings behind it.

That it was becoming harder and harder for him to imagine his life without her. That such a thought caused a pain inside he'd not experienced even in war. An indescribable void of self-induced suffering.

What was becoming obvious the more time he spent with Ashlyn was that he wasn't meant to be alone. He was meant to be with people. He felt better with her than without her. Being with her, he thought, for the first time, that he could do the mental work he needed to do. Not that she was a panacea for his psychiatric difficulties, but in partnership, they could both be better together than they were apart.

Liam pulled his head back and looked into her eyes. She held his gaze. He brushed a smudge of dirt off her face.

"Thank you," Liam said.

"For what?"

"For staying with me. For bringing me back to you."

He caught just a hint of her perfume. "I need to fix something."

"What?" Her voice was barely a whisper— breathless…wanting.

"I want our first kiss to be something not brought on by danger but by meaning. I don't want it to feel like a mistake…an act of desperation to connect me with reality."

He leaned forward. Her breath puffed warm against his cheek. He brushed her nose with his… teasing. "I want you to know that I mean it."

Liam pressed his lips against hers and then cupped her head with his hands, pulling her lips to his. A soft sigh escaped her lips, and when he rested his palm against her neck, he could feel her pulse racing against his skin. She wrapped her arms around his back and pulled him closer against herself. His finger traced her neckline, and she wilted into his arms.

"All right, you two. You've survived death and had a little celebration about it. We're ready to let you go. Sheriff Black vouched for you and verified your…conundrum."

Liam reluctantly peeled away, and Ashlyn held his gaze. "That kiss will definitely be more memorable."

The town of Rock Springs, Wyoming, was only partly aptly named. There were rocks… lots of them of varying sizes and shapes, but not a lot of water to be seen. Some of the rock formations were wonderful, and if they weren't so exhausted and living on a knife's edge, Ashlyn would have loved to spend some time taking in the historical landmarks.

Instead, each of them reclined on a twin bed in a low-budget motel off the beaten path. A newly minted Sweetwater County sheriff's deputy had driven them to Rock Springs.

"Three," Ashlyn said.

"Three what?" Liam asked.

"Maybe four."

"Want to give me a hint of what you're talking about?"

Ashlyn laughed. The language of men and women was so different, but she was also trying to be intentionally vague. They were stuck here for the night until they could hit a local car dealership in the morning for another old set of wheels, likely no more charming than the last vehicle they'd trotted across the country in.

"Law enforcement agencies that we've had to give statements to," Ashlyn said.

"Technically only three. I think the handoff to Sweetwater County was just to get us out of the hair of Sublette County. Sublette was kind enough to get our kind of trouble out of their boundary lines."

The other numbers Ashlyn didn't want to think too much about. How many people had tried to complete the contract? How many were still on the hunt, hoping for the payoff? Was Mackenzie alive? Were Doc, Dolores and Emory okay? Intentionally, they weren't carrying cell phones, but that didn't seem to dissuade the trackers enough.

"Do you think much about Claire? A sister you never knew about?" Liam asked.

"I've been thinking about her a lot. It's easy to

live a fantasy life when you don't come from a stable home. If you imagine something enough, then I think it's easier to bring it about in normal life."

Liam seemed deep in thought as he stared up at the ceiling. What she hoped he was thinking through was a different life from the one he was living. Could he create a life with the two of them together? With children? If he thought about it enough, would he want to bring it to fruition?

"Would you change it? Your upbringing?" Liam asked.

It was easy to say yes. But if she traded in the hard experiences for a home with two loving parents and never wanting for anything… she would not be the same person she was now. She would have never met Liam.

"Painful experiences make us who we are. I know you asked me this before, about how God could allow evil if He was good, but I think if there weren't the bad things that happened in our lives, we would never look to God for comfort, either. At least for me personally, going through bad times forced me to reach to Him for guidance and comfort. I think if we're given free choice, then God has to allow for the consequences, but He remains with us as we deal with them."

Liam was quiet. She glanced over his way. He turned on his side, away from her. It killed her that he didn't respond to her thoughts on his question, but if she'd learned anything as a nurse in working with patients, sometimes a person just needed to ruminate over what was said to conclude on their own. Continuing to talk to them would not help them reach any sort of decision.

Would Liam ever get to where he could trust her with all his thoughts and feelings? If not, she couldn't imagine a way they could have a relationship with each other.

# TWELVE

Liam counted the amount of cash he had left. He wasn't worried yet, but if he didn't haggle this guy down on the price of this bedraggled truck by another thousand, then he'd have to figure out a way to get additional funds without drawing attention. Paying in cash seemed to convince the man to accept Liam's price, and they loaded their few belongings into the open bed. He took stock of what Ashlyn and he were wearing. Though able to sleep through the night and shower this morning, both remained in the same clothes they'd survived the vehicle rollover in. Trouble was that car crash jeans and ripped winter coats were going to do nothing more than draw attention to themselves. They'd need new clothing.

"We need to make a quick stop," Liam said as he climbed into the driver's seat.

Ashlyn secured her seat belt. "For?"

"Clothes. We show up in Fort Collins looking like this and they'll think we just crawled out of the deep woods after hibernating for a few months. We don't need extra attention or questions."

"You're going to take a girl clothes shopping?"

"I mean…one outfit and not too spendy." Liam found the familiar blue-and-white sign with a yellow star. Their new truck ran more smoothly than it looked, and he eased into a parking space. "I'll buy you a high-priced coffee if you can make your selections in under ten."

"Ten minutes?"

"Well, I was thinking ten seconds…" He turned to her and winked. They piled out of the vehicle and entered the store. Liam flashed his watch at Ashlyn and motioned to the registers. She nodded.

Liam headed toward the gun counter. They needed more ammunition, and it would be easier to get a few more weapons in Wyoming than in Colorado. He turned the corner and stopped in his tracks.

Douglas stood at the counter talking to a salesman.

*What's he doing here? So far away from Jackson Hole?*

Interesting thing about his brother was he was anti-gun. As far as Liam knew, he didn't own a piece of weaponry. Douglas's preferred lethal antidotes were legal loopholes, and he was good at finding them and cutting people off at the knees without so much as a drop of spilled blood.

Liam's nerves zinged. Was it better to confront the enemy or stay in stealth mode and see what developed of the situation? Had anyone come into the store with his brother? This was probably the safest place to garner new information. The coincidence was likely not any such prospect. The only thing in this direction was the unknown element of Mackenzie's long-lost sister. The ransom note had given no location where to exchange the money for Mackenzie—if she were truly still alive. Did Douglas have some knowledge he hadn't shared with law enforcement? Had he had further communication with Mackenzie's presumed kidnapper? Were Wesley Taylor and the FBI out of the loop?

Was Douglas trying to rescue Mackenzie?

Only one way to find out. Tackle the problem with a frontal assault.

Liam walked up to the counter and leaned on the glass case with his elbow. Douglas sensed the movement and turned in Liam's direction, and the gun he held slipped from his hands onto the glass-topped surface.

"Big brother," Liam said. "Last place I thought I'd see you was in Rock Springs, Wyoming."

Douglas swallowed hard. His eyes shifted from side to side—the wheels of his mind turning to spin a tale. Liam couldn't wait to hear what it was.

"I…have an event here today."

Interesting. If he were helping to find Mackenzie, why not admit it? What was he hiding? Liam wished he could fact-check the truthfulness of the statement by pulling out his cell phone and scrolling through the local events. No such luck.

"Is there a threat to your life now? I didn't think you liked to handle guns," Liam said, emphasizing the note of sarcasm in his voice.

"Can't be too careful," Douglas said. "Considering all that's happened, I decided it would be best to take extra measures."

"Are you heading into Colorado?" Liam asked.

Douglas's lack of a quick response belied whatever he was going to say next. "No plans to."

"I just know that buying guns in Wyoming is a lot easier than in the neighboring state."

"Guess that's why you're here, then, as well," Douglas said.

"Is there any recent news on Mackenzie? Another ransom note delivered?"

Douglas handed his credit card to the salesman. "Nothing that has been shared. The investigators aren't talking to me."

"That happens when you're a person of interest. They cut you out. You know, what I find interesting—"

"Can't imagine, little brother," Douglas interrupted dismissively.

"—is why you haven't asked me what I'm doing here and why mentioning Colorado doesn't surprise you. I'm wondering if we could be heading to the same place."

Douglas turned and faced him. "I don't have any business in Colorado."

"You're not visiting a woman who claims to be Mackenzie's sister?"

The news didn't surprise Douglas—though he tried to cover the lack thereof with his words. "I wasn't aware Mackenzie had a sister other than Ashlyn. It's not something she told me. Probably someone trying to get money from her. You'd be surprised how many people want to be in our sphere of influence for cash and favors."

"Maybe if they knew the two of you were connected, which, thus far, you haven't been very public about. Plus, it's hard to get money from a woman who's missing. Not hard to get it from someone who might want her back. If he wants her back."

Douglas took his credit card back from the salesman. "What are you saying?"

"Seems to me like you're doing one of two

things. You're trying to save Mackenzie or you're trying to tie up loose ends. I happen to think the latter."

"If you have proof of my misdeeds, then give it to the police." Douglas set his hand on the gun, which the salesman had packaged. "You've always been more trouble than you're worth, Liam."

"I wouldn't be any trouble to you if you took the contract down on Ashlyn's life. If you helped me find Mackenzie."

Douglas's eye twitched. "Good luck to you. Hope you find what you're looking for." He grabbed the package and hurried away.

"Can I help you, sir?" the salesman asked.

"Yeah... I need a couple of boxes of ammo for a SIG Sauer. Make it four. Can't ever have too much these days."

"Might as well grab enough while it's in stock. Supply chains aren't what they used to be."

"Do you know that man?" Liam asked.

"No, sir," the man said as he took out the boxes from the locked cabinet.

"Mind if I borrow your phone? Just want to see if there's something fun going on locally to take in before we leave the area."

The man put in his password and handed the phone over. "Sure, but I don't think much is going on around here until New Year's Eve. Things are winding down after Christmas."

Liam pulled up the internet search engine and entered Douglas's name and Rock Springs.

No events listed.

Ashlyn looked at the clock on the wall. Fifteen minutes had passed. She had dressed in the new clothes with the tags in her hand, waiting for Liam to show up by the registers. She would definitely insist on two high-priced coffees at this rate.

Another five minutes passed before Liam made his way over.

"Did you see him?" he immediately asked her, taking the tags from her hands.

"Who?"

"Douglas."

"Here?"

"At the gun counter."

Ashlyn's stomach sank. She could see her reaction played out in Liam's mirrored sunglasses. "You talked to him?"

"Tried to. Asked him if he knew about Claire. He denied it, of course. Douglas is going to Colorado to either get Mackenzie or cover for his crimes. Unfortunately, I don't think it's for your sister, because he's not working with law enforcement. Right now, they probably don't have enough to hold him."

"I don't think Douglas is trying to save Mackenzie, either," Ashlyn agreed. "We need to figure out the ransom piece. Who has Mackenzie and why are they holding her? Hopefully, Claire will have the answer."

"Exactly." Liam rubbed his hand over his face. He paced to a self-checkout and scanned the tags quickly. The beeping intensified the sick feeling in Ashlyn's gut. She could see Liam mentally clicking through their options and she guessed none was better than the other.

If they left now in daylight and took the most traveled road, they'd be found for sure. Waiting until dark and traveling less conspicuous roads wasn't a great idea, either. Considering the distance between here and Fort Collins, traveling on the roads wasn't safe anymore.

"I have a buddy that lives in the area. We can't risk the roads anymore. Not with Douglas close. If he's behind the contracts, he's already updated all the mercenaries as to our location. I'm going to see if my friend will fly us into Fort Collins. Plus, we need to try and get ahead of my brother."

He walked up to the local cashier and asked to borrow her phone.

It was early morning the next day, five days after Christmas. Ashlyn and Liam sat outside Claire Brown's house in a dodgy, rusted-out, new-to-them purchased car. Liam had convinced the car salesman in Rock Springs to give him his money back for the truck—less a five-hundred-dollar processing fee. A generous return for an hour of his time. Ever since the flight from Rock Springs, Wyoming, to Fort Collins, Colorado, Ashlyn's body hovered in a hypervigilant state. Each unexpected sound caused her nerves to fire. Even a reassuring touch from Liam caused her to jump and reach for the door's handle to flee.

*Maybe I've been expecting too much from Liam. If this is how I feel after a few days of some sloppily trained men coming after me— what must it be like to have trained killers wholly armed coming after you day after day? Living with the memories of not always being able to save the people you so hoped you could make a difference to? Lord, I ask Your forgiveness for my expectations of Liam. I don't know and can't even come to the subtlest of understanding about the experiences he's had that have injured his mind. If this experience gives me an ounce of what he's experienced these last few years, then I thank You for that. Help me understand him better.*

What was it that people said…about walking a mile in someone's shoes? She knew now she couldn't have lived where Liam had and survived, and she felt guilty for expecting him to be further along in the healing process than he was. Liam felt he was doing what was safe for him and others. She didn't begrudge patients when they didn't follow the game plan. If they returned because of the effects of whatever illness and not following the prescribed treatment, she always tried to give compassionate care. Yet she wasn't giving Liam the same time or space. To maintain personal health, boundaries had to be set up and respected. This was when nurses got into trouble in relationships. Caring people were the most apt to get into negative, codependent places with people who weren't ready to do the work to heal.

Where did that put her and Liam? If he was this affected by his PTSD to the point something did not always ground him in reality—clearly needing treatment but refusing—it may not be caring or smart to continue to facilitate that.

"Movement."

She startled and quickly rubbed her hands against her thighs to soothe her troubled nerves. Focusing on the front of the house, she saw two women emerge with a child in a wheelchair. The older woman was presumably Claire Brown, the younger perhaps an aide. The child appeared to be elementary school age, but certain disease processes made it difficult to judge age accurately. They waited for the women to load the child into the handicapped van and pull out. After they were a few yards down the road, Liam put the car into Drive and followed.

Ashlyn chastised herself for not noticing the signs earlier. The handicap ramp to the residence. The special assistance van sitting in the driveway. Maybe Ashlyn ignored the obvious because she hoped another child wasn't afflicted with what Emory had. Or to the extent Emory could be. Seeing the girl was a paved road for what could become of Emory.

The same autosomal dominant muscle wasting disease.

"So Claire does have a child," Liam stated.

"Appears so."

"Is this what Emory has in store for her?" Liam asked.

"If Emory gets a full expression of the disease, it will be if there's no cure."

"Explain it to me—what the disease is."

"It's a ticking time bomb. If you carry an autosomal dominant trait, you have a fifty-fifty chance of spreading it to your offspring. Sometimes, with diseases passed genetically, the expression in each person is different."

"How do you know who will get the worst case?" Liam asked.

"You don't. The disease process can highly

affect some individuals and others may have very mild to no obvious symptoms. They call this *penetrance*, and no one can predict how affected an individual will be with the disease until they express it."

"There's no way to prepare yourself beforehand, then."

Ashlyn nodded. "Exactly. Sometimes the penetrance might be worse in alternating generations, which could explain why Claire and Mackenzie don't have any evidence of the disease, but their children, or at least Claire's child, are showing symptoms. Claire and Mackenzie might also be full siblings—twins, even, as you noted. I don't know enough about my parents to know if we all have the same father."

Claire turned into an office lot and parked in one of the handicap spaces. Liam parked toward the back of the lot. The signage signified that it provided outpatient therapy.

"I think seeing Claire with this sick child answers our remaining questions. I think when Claire reached out to Mackenzie, she learned about the cure and she's trying to get it. What mother wouldn't do anything necessary to save her child? Even if it means criminal activity."

Ashlyn swallowed past a lump in her throat. The quick demise of Mackenzie's first child, Emory's older sibling, had been a surprise to both her and her sister. The doctors had called it a fluke—a one-in-a-million happenstance—this unknown disease that at the time they couldn't identify. Even though Ashlyn had been part of these conversations with families when they were delivered a devastating diagnosis, it didn't matter to those parents if the rarest of events was happening to them when it ended in the death of their child.

Something had always bothered Mackenzie about Emory's sibling's death, and she'd insisted on an autopsy and genetic testing. That was when they'd first found out about the genetic mutation. So much more was known now about the human genome after the entirety of the human chromosome had been mapped out. When Mackenzie had herself tested, they found the same mutation, but without also studying the older sibling's father, it couldn't be known if it was an autosomal recessive or dominant disease process. The difference between those two things was that for the 50 percent chance expression in a dominant transmission, only one parent had to be affected. For a recessive trait to be passed on, both parents had to be carriers.

Mackenzie had hoped that the genetic transmission was the less risky one when she became pregnant with Emory. Whether unfortunate or otherwise, Mackenzie had tested Emory at birth, and they'd found the same genetic mutation. That lent to the autosomal dominant transmission theory, and now that Claire's child seemed to have some muscular deficiency affliction as well, dominant transmission was the most likely reason the illness was being passed on.

Ashlyn's chances of having this genetic trait were the same as Mackenzie's if they shared the same two parents. A fifty-fifty chance.

"Do you know if you're a carrier?" Liam asked.

Ashlyn had wondered how long it would take Liam to ask this question. How could she be frustrated with him when she hadn't tackled her own medical mystery? "I haven't…been brave enough to yet."

He nodded in response, keeping his eyes on the building.

Ashlyn continued. "I guess I didn't feel that I needed to worry about it until I met someone who was interested in having children."

The statement hung in the air of the car, and Liam's lack of response plummeted Ashlyn's heart through the floorboards. To be fair, his question had been heavy-handed and this wasn't a great time to delve into it. Liam was not unaware of the feelings that were growing between them. His actions showed more resistance to the idea of building a long-term relationship than giving indications he was wholeheartedly in it to move forward. A kiss wasn't a guarantee of a lifelong commitment.

"Do you want children? Of your own?" Liam asked, drumming his fingers against the steering wheel.

Ashlyn looked at him. Her mind hummed with the possibilities of his statement. "Yes, I want to have my own family. Do you?"

"What if that never happens for you?" Liam asked. "Would you be happy with your life?"

The question stunned her. *What does he mean? I'm young. Of course I'll have those things.*

Liam continued. "I know it's what you want, but in all your talk about God providing for you...about living in His will—what if that's not His plan for you? Would you be okay with that?"

She swallowed hard. How could Liam even ask such a thing? Of course this was what God wanted for her. How could He want anything different?

"Are you depending wholly on God for all your needs, or are you trying to force something that's not in His will?"

Ashlyn responded defensively. "For someone who's not too sure about God, you seem to be spouting a lot about how I should be living my life."

"Ashlyn," he said, his words soft, "these are the things *you've* told me."

She slammed her gaping mouth shut and closed her eyes. His observation was a dagger to her gut and a dull ache fluttered out. What if what she wanted wasn't God's plan? How could that be determined? What if Liam wasn't supposed to be part of her life? What if children presumably wouldn't be part of it? Was she wishing for something she shouldn't? Was she asking to live outside of God's will in her desire to have those things?

Liam's words filled the quiet space. "I never really considered the possibility of a wife, let alone children. I'm not sure I'd be safe around them."

"You've never hurt me," Ashlyn said, on the verge of tears.

"Maybe we've just been fortunate that I haven't." Liam raked his fingers through his beard. He couldn't look her way. "What if I had mistaken you for an enemy on the battlefield instead of my friend?" *Friend?* The word…a death knell for any relationship. "Who knows what I would do then?"

So that was it…the ultimate basis of Liam's fear. That he'd mistake her for someone he meant to do harm to and wouldn't be able to tell the difference. The thought wasn't heartwarming, but his actions—those times when he disassociated from reality—hadn't led to any such event. Many smart people said the best predictor of future behavior was what people had shown in the past.

Liam's actions had always saved her from harm. Not put her in harm's way.

"If you put all that fear aside and knew you could be healed…or at least come to a place where PTSD didn't rule your life…could you see yourself having children?" she asked.

Liam dismissed her question and pointed to the front of the building. "They're back out."

Ashlyn checked her watch. A full forty-five minutes had passed. Where had the time gone?

Instead of heading straight to the van, Claire was pushing the child's wheelchair to a nearby park. The assistant followed. Ashlyn grabbed the door handle and opened it.

"What are you going to do?"

"I'm going to talk to her."

Liam's mouth popped open. No words came forth.

"Do you have another suggestion?" Ashlyn asked.

"No. I'm just not sure if I should go with you or not."

"They'll probably be more willing to talk to a woman alone than one approaching them with a man they don't recognize."

"All right, but I'm keeping my eye on you."

# THIRTEEN

Ashlyn exited the car. Was this a smart move? Probably not. She didn't know this woman and didn't know if her reaching out to Mackenzie had been for nefarious reasons or not. What she knew was that she needed space from Liam. For one moment, she didn't want to think about him and their relationship, or the possibility of it, if there even was such a thing happening now.

Closing the door behind her, she inhaled the cool, bitter air of the frosted afternoon. Over the horizon of the mountains, a gathering of dark clouds portended a coming storm. The wind picked up, an echo of the forthcoming tempest, and whipped Ashlyn's hair into her face. Pulling it aside, she could see that Claire and the other woman had settled on a bench with the girl's wheelchair parked next to them.

How did you approach a woman that you needed information from, one who didn't know how dire the situation was?

Ashlyn glanced behind her. Liam had stepped out of the car and was leaning against the hood, watching her movements.

She walked toward the duo and sat next to the woman she presumed to be Claire. She looked older than her biological age if she was Mackenzie's twin—somewhere in her late thirties or early forties. Her hair was nearly fully gray and pulled back in a tight braid. Eyes a pale, milky brown. Face wrinkled like a woman twice her age. Sturdy muscles from the physical labor of caring for her daughter. "I'm Ashlyn."

The woman didn't answer immediately. She pulled a snack out of a backpack and placed a smattering of brightly colored rice puffs on the tray for the girl to eat. "I wondered how long it would be before you found me."

Ashlyn's heart leaped into her throat. She placed her hand over her neck to hide the pounding. The flow of adrenaline through her body charged her senses. "You know me?"

"I know *of* you. Mackenzie wasn't silent about your existence."

Ashlyn crossed her legs and kicked her foot furiously as she thought through her next move. She wanted to charge forward with the information she really needed to know, but couldn't anticipate how a line of direct questioning would make Claire feel. She didn't want to scare her off before she had any valuable information.

"Is this your daughter?" Ashlyn asked.

"I didn't kidnap her."

Ashlyn frowned. The response was strange. The slight edge to her words hinted at a subdued hostility. As if Ashlyn's presence was oxygen to a smoldering fire of anger.

"She's beautiful," Ashlyn said.

"Eyes just like Mackenzie, wouldn't you say?"

Ashlyn didn't respond. The conversation was taking a turn down a dark road. The air between them was charged with something foreign, and Ashlyn didn't know if she trusted the position she put herself in. Relief washed over her, knowing that Liam was there keeping tabs on the situation. Claire glanced around the park, almost as if she was looking for something… or someone.

Claire dug her keys out of her pocket. "Sara, why don't you take Zoe over for her swim therapy. I'll meet you there in a bit." The younger woman took the keys from Claire's hand, not asking how Claire would get there herself, and pushed the child away.

"Your daughter is sick with the same disease that Emory has. That her older brother died of," Ashlyn stated.

"Why are you here?" Claire asked when the

two were out of earshot. "You here on behalf of Douglas? He going to pay up after all?"

Ashlyn inhaled sharply. Time for the offensive. "Hasn't he already paid some? Zoe got Emory's cure, didn't she?"

"Only part of it. And he owes me a lot more than that."

"Like the ransom payout," Ashlyn added.

"Ding-ding-ding." The words were mocking, filled with disdain. Ashlyn's gut grew heavy. Something wasn't right. The sky dimmed as clouds passed over the lowering sun.

"Mackenzie kept a journal. She said you had reached out to her through one of those DNA websites."

"Not much a mother won't do when her child is dying from a terminal illness."

Did that include murder? At the very least, kidnapping for ransom? Many parents faced losing a child and didn't resort to violence as a means to an end.

"You don't remember me, do you?" Claire said.

"I don't remember much about my younger years. Just getting bounced from foster home to foster home."

"You should ask yourself why that is," Claire said.

"You and Mackenzie are full siblings."

"Twins. Mackenzie got everything, and I got nothin' but a sick kid and bills I can't pay."

What did Claire mean? She'd been the one adopted out and given a home. Ashlyn could understand the financial strain of having a terminally ill child. Bills mounted quickly and there were diminishing resources that families could tap into, particularly as their children grew older.

"Where is Mackenzie?"

Claire smirked. Ashlyn saw movement behind a nearby tree and the hairs at the base of her neck prickled. Was this another person trying to cash in on the contract? Her common sense told her it was time to leave, but she disregarded the instinct. Whatever danger was coming was worth sticking around for if it helped her find her sister. Perhaps surviving all that she'd been through in the preceding days was giving her a sense of bravado she shouldn't claim.

"Mackenzie always wanted to protect you," Claire said.

"What did you mean when you said that Mackenzie got everything and you didn't?"

Claire let out a short, maniacal laugh. "Who is living on an expensive property in Jackson Hole, Wyoming? Who is connected to the next big name in Wyoming politics? Who finagled her way into funding the cure for this disease and then wanted to keep it all to herself?"

"We also spent our childhood in foster care," Ashlyn said.

"Some families are worse than the system." Ashlyn swallowed.

"Mackenzie didn't want to share the cure with you?"

"She was hoarding what was available for Emory even though her daughter isn't even sick right now. Had to twist arms to get it. At least the first installment, as they say. Douglas did fund research to find a cure for Emory. With all the research into these new types of vaccines, the private lab Douglas hired theorized these new mRNA immunizations can give the cells a recipe to have them manufacture the protein the body needs to…cheat this disease. I paid someone at the lab for some inside intel. What's another five thousand when you're close to a quarter million in debt."

Ashlyn motioned to the outpatient building. "The treatment your daughter just received is a theory based on the success of one successful vaccine and nothing more. You don't know that it will work."

"Desperate people do desperate things. What could be worse than what Zoe is living through now? She can hardly feed herself finger foods."

This was always a sticky situation. Parents with special-needs kids were some of the strongest people out there. The ethical questions that surrounded their children's care were never easy. What was a good choice for one family could devastate another.

"Where are you holding Mackenzie?" Ashlyn asked again.

"If you pay her ransom, I'll tell you."

"She's still alive?"

"She is…for now."

"How can I save her?" Ashlyn asked.

"Do you trust Douglas?"

"Of course not."

"Then you shouldn't trust me, either."

Before Ashlyn could blink, Claire pulled a handgun from her tote bag and was pointing it at her.

Then a figure emerged from behind the trees.

"Can't have you saving your sister until I get my money…or some money. I can fulfill Douglas's contract on your life just as well as someone else. And the payment will be automatic."

Liam pushed away from the car as he saw a figure move into the open space. The man had a weapon pulled and was straight-lining it for Ashlyn. At the same moment, Ashlyn grabbed Claire's arm, and the two wrestled. Liam pulled his own weapon and could feel his mind drift from reality. He couldn't lose touch with the present. Ashlyn's life depended on him staying centered.

*No...no...no! Please, God. If You really are there and You are for me, then I need You to keep me here. Please, for Ashlyn's sake...for her life.*

Liam narrowed his eyes and focused on the variables. The man was closing the distance quickly. Ashlyn had somehow wrestled the gun from Claire and thrown it off to the side and was bear-hugging Claire to keep her arms pinned. Liam ran forward, his weapon trained on the unknown assailant's head.

"Drop the gun—now!"

The man looked his way, but barely flinched. He kept eye contact with Claire and then took a stance a mere foot away from Ashlyn, who was struggling to hold Claire from going for the gun. If the assailant leaned forward, he could press the barrel against Ashlyn's forehead. Icy fear poured into Liam's veins, but his fingertips pulsed hot against the trigger. Liam was surprised at Ashlyn's fortitude, keeping Claire contained with a weapon trained on her.

Liam stopped a few feet away from the gunman and broadened his stance. "I said, put the weapon down."

"Seems like we have ourselves a stalemate," the gunman said.

"This is a public area in the middle of daylight. It will not take someone too long to see us and call the police," Liam said.

"I got nothing left to live for. I either get my money or I die today—either is fine with me," the man responded.

"What about jail? If you kill anyone here, I'll incapacitate you enough for the police to make an arrest, and you'll spend a lot of time there."

"Three squares a day is better than what I'm getting now."

Men living under desperate circumstances were the most dangerous. When they had thought through all the options and were fine with each choice, no matter how dire they were, there was little ability to bargain.

"I think we can solve this before anyone gets hurt," Claire said.

Liam could see the debate in Ashlyn's eyes— was it better to let Claire go or hold on? Ashlyn glanced behind her where the gun had landed in the mulch and decided it was better to keep her contained. *Good choice, Ashlyn.* Holding Claire close might prohibit the gunman from firing if he and Claire were working together, and she owed him money. Liam couldn't be sure that was the case. Who knew what other contracts could be out there awaiting payment?

"Mackenzie doesn't have long to live," Claire said. The news was enough for Ashlyn to loosen her grip and for Claire to scurry away, but Claire didn't sidle up to the unknown assailant for protection, which puzzled Liam. Neither woman went for the gun. Whose team was Claire on? Was the gunman not there at her behest?

Then a wail escaped Claire's lips. Ashlyn shuddered and innately reached out to comfort her. Claire slapped her hand away. "What would you pay to save your child's life?" she screamed. "All I want is for Zoe to be cured. *Fully cured.* Is that too much to ask for? I thought grabbing Douglas's precious mistress and holding her for ransom would force him to give it to me. Turns out he cares nothing about Mackenzie. He'd rather see her dead."

Liam advanced a few inches. If he could get within striking range of the unknown element and subdue him, Ashlyn could handle Claire if she tried to go for the weapon.

"What are you talking about?" Ashlyn asked.

Claire shifted her eyes to Liam. "You're him, aren't you? The navy SEAL who came back all messed up in the head from overseas. Douglas talks about you all the time and how weak you are. How *broken and useless you've become.*"

The words seethed from her mouth like a snake hissing. Claire faced the gunman. "Just shoot him! I'll take care of her."

*"I don't work for you,"* the man said.

A breeze rustled through the trees. Its chill and the man's statement caused Liam's heart to stutter a few beats. Liam's head swam. Claire's venomous words spread through his veins, and he weakened beneath the weight of their truth.

Liam consciously straightened his shoulders, fighting against the toxic thoughts, and focused his eyes back on Claire. He would not allow playground taunting from a woman he didn't even know to unhinge him from reality.

At the gunman's confession, Claire lifted her hands in the air in surrender.

"I didn't place a death contract out on anyone's life. I did…arrange for Mackenzie's kidnapping. My plan was to hold her until I'm given what I need for my daughter from Douglas. If you want to know who is putting out all these hits," Claire said, pointing to Liam, "you need to look no further than your own brother."

Sadly, this news was no surprise for Liam.

"It was Douglas that decided to off Mackenzie and the baby. Mackenzie was making too many demands on him, and he was fed up with it. I just happened to get to Mackenzie before Douglas did. And a good thing, because then

I would have never gotten what I needed for Zoe. Douglas first assumed when Mackenzie went missing that the contract on her life had been fulfilled. When he saw from the cameras that Ashlyn had the baby, he put up the contract for her."

Liam swallowed hard. He was losing hope that his brother could ever be redeemed.

"Douglas made it clear he wasn't going to pay me the ransom. He wanted her dead all along anyway. Douglas found my original ransom note at Mackenzie's house. I knew he would go there to get Mackenzie's journal. To cover his tracks, Douglas blew up the whole house to get rid of any other evidence. Stuff he's paranoid about that may not even exist. He's still probably got that first note somewhere."

"The red envelope," Liam confirmed.

"Exactly. I had a second ransom demand delivered to put pressure on him, knowing the police, or some other party, would find it."

Claire held her phone up for all of them to see. "Douglas confessed everything to me, and I have it all recorded. If he didn't bring me the cure for Zoe, I was going to use the information to expose him to the police and get what I wanted that way. *I never intended for anyone to die.*"

Liam's thoughts were tumultuous. He quickly

calculated the new variable through his mind as he grieved what his brother had become. Douglas was a cold, heartless puppet master, and he didn't care what crimes he committed as long as he got his way. If Douglas wasn't implicated in these crimes, then he could pursue his political goals, and who knew what untoward power he would ruthlessly use once he got into higher office. This information could mean several things.

The gunman wasn't here to kill Ashlyn.

He was there to kill Claire.

Claire had figured this out as well. Douglas was tying up loose ends.

And as Liam decided in his mind to take out the gunman, a shot rang out. Without looking at what damage the bullet had wrought, Liam discharged his firearm, bringing down the assailant with a wound to the leg. The man dropped his gun and clenched his knee. Liam advanced to his position and kicked his weapon several yards away. Blood sluiced from the wound. Liam placed two hands over the man's leg to help control the bleeding and looked in Ashlyn's direction.

*Please, Lord, let her be alive.*

A warm mist sprayed over Ashlyn's face. She reached up to wipe the droplets away and brought her fingers down, a flash of red in her eyes. Claire crumpled to the ground. Ashlyn jumped from the bench and crawled to her. Blood plumed up and saturated Claire's clothing to her left chest. Claire was conscious, her eyes wide with fear.

"It's okay," Ashlyn said, though only half-heartedly believing it. She pushed up Claire's winter vest and shirt and noticed a wound to the rib cage on the left side. It was lower than the level of her heart, but a bullet could ricochet wildly once it hit bone. There were plenty of important structures other than the heart that, if injured, could still lead to death. The whisper of sirens arced in the wind. Likely law enforcement over medical personnel.

"This is going to hurt," Ashlyn said as she pressed two hands against the gunshot wound.

Claire cried out and grabbed Ashlyn's hand. "I'm not…going to…make it."

The choppy words indicated difficulty breathing. A collapsed lung could be one of the primary causes. "You will," Ashlyn assured her.

Claire shook her head. "Listen…to me." She floppily groped the ground for the phone that had fallen from her hand when she was shot. Pulling it up, she shoved it into Ashlyn's chest. "It's all here." She slapped her hand rapidly against Ashlyn's forearm. "Keep it."

Ashlyn noted the blue tinge to Claire's lips. A sign of her body's lack of oxygen. Ashlyn looked at the ground and noticed the trails of blood seeping from underneath Claire's body.

"Stay with me," Ashlyn ordered.

"Evidence…is there." Her breathing became rapid. "Don't trust…anyone. Our…birthday."

Ashlyn grabbed the phone and slipped it into her pocket. The sirens grew closer. Liam rushed to her and pulled her from Claire.

"We've got to go…now."

"No! I can't leave her."

"Ashlyn, we've got to move." He pulled her to a standing position.

She pushed him away from her. "I'm not leaving her!"

Liam grabbed her arms and pulled her close. "If we have any chance of saving Mackenzie, we've got to go now. If we're detained by the police, it's going to be hours, and no one is going to believe this tale. This crime spree is going to take months, if not years, to sort out. We can't be held in police custody. Your sister, if still alive, likely won't be for long."

Ashlyn was pulled as Liam hustled her from the park. They went a few yards into the woods and hid. Within minutes, police swarmed the park, followed by EMS.

"What are we going to do?"

"You have Claire's phone and I know where Douglas will go."

"Where?"

"If he's in cleanup mode...we need to get to Claire's house. My guess is he'll go there to destroy evidence. Same as he tried to do at Mackenzie's."

Liam pulled Ashlyn away from the scene. "Hopefully, those officers will first think those two shot each other. Both of them aren't going to be talking a lot in the short term."

None of this felt good or right. Another peal of sirens. Even though morally she was having difficulty running away from the situation, she knew Liam was right: there wasn't anything she could do for Claire now.

She followed Liam as he traversed through the woods.

# FOURTEEN

The park where Ashlyn had confronted Claire was a mile from Claire's house. Inherently, Liam had developed a good sense of direction through his military training. He could visualize a topographical view and was able to wind them through back roads until they reached the alley behind Claire's house. After hopping the split-rail fence, Liam tested the sliding back door and found it unlocked.

They hustled inside. Liam locked the door and pulled the vertical blinds closed. The house smelled of a multitude of cats mixed with the antiseptic smell of medical equipment. Liam's stomach turned, the odor and not having eaten recently wreaking havoc.

"Claire's phone," Liam said, holding his hand out.

Ashlyn pulled it from her pocket and slid her thumb up the screen, bringing up the number pad for the pass code.

He looked at her quizzically. "Any guesses?"

"Claire said one strange thing to me about 'our birthday.'"

Liam typed in Ashlyn's birthday and the numbers cleared from the screen. "No go."

"You remember when my birthday is?"

Heat flushed Liam's face. It was a day he often looked forward to. He'd never been one to send her birthday cards as she did him, but he always thought of her on that day. Not a time to be discussing it anyway. "What other birthday could she mean?"

Ashlyn crossed her arms over her chest. "Claire and Mackenzie are twins."

"What's your sister's birthday?"

Ashlyn grabbed the phone from him and typed it in. The phone unlocked. "We need to get to the audio files she talked about."

"Let me scan through them. I know deception better than you do. I know my brother Douglas. You look around here and see if you can find anything that might give us a hint where Claire might have stashed Mackenzie until the ransom was paid."

Liam pulled a seat from the cluttered kitchen table and sat down. There were several audio files. He opened the most recent one, recorded yesterday. Liam noted the time stamp. It was right after he'd seen Douglas at the store buying a weapon. Wind whipped in the background. Douglas must have called from outside. Maybe the reason Liam hadn't seen him was that he was hiding to the side or back of the building, making this phone call.

Claire: "I'm not giving you the address where Mackenzie is until you get me an appointment with the doctor who has the cure."

Douglas: "I told you I will bring the cure to you. Arrangements have already been made. I'm already halfway to Fort Collins."

Claire: "And what will I do with whatever you give me, not knowing how to administer it? I need to meet with the doctor. I need to know he'll agree to treat Zoe."

Douglas: "You're asking for more than we agreed to. I told you I'd bring you the cure, and you'd tell me where Mackenzie is."

Claire: "I'm not as stupid as you take me for. I want an appointment with the doctor. That has to happen before I give you any information about Mackenzie."

Douglas: "That will not happen. Honestly, this entire plan of yours is benefiting me. Do you think I care about what happens to Mackenzie and her ilk? Why do you think I set fire to her house in her absence? Partly to cover my own crimes but also so she'd have nothing to come back to. A woman I had a relationship with has been blackmailing me for this cure for a year. Is that love? Having Mackenzie disappear will only help me politically. The more I think about this, the more I say…do whatever you want with Mackenzie. I'm cleaning up things on my end. Even if you release Mackenzie, the crime of her going missing falls squarely on your shoulders. You forget, I have the ransom note you left me all preserved and awaiting forensics. I'll make all the papers welcoming Mackenzie back. Admitting my mistakes will woo people to cast their votes for me. And curing Emory of a deadly illness in the name of love will win me the governorship of my state. I think our business is done."

Claire: "You'll go to jail. I've been taping our conversations. One email of these audio files to the FBI and you're finished. You'll be lucky if you ever see the outside of a jail cell your remaining days."

A string of expletives followed. The spider caught in his own trap. What Douglas hadn't counted into his equation was the life that Claire had led. Getting the scraps of what she considered leftovers had prepared her for this moment. Likely, Claire had lived a life on the edge. Even Ashlyn alluded to wanting the safety and security of a family. Moving from home to home, it was easy to develop a feeling of being discarded by society. Whereas Ashlyn had used her experiences to wish for something more secure and safe, Claire's adopted family had evidently shown her life through the lens where no one could be trusted, and she operated with that baseline understanding. Nothing would be given to her. She'd have to take it.

Douglas: "I'll make arrangements. Two days' time. Another doctor, closely connected with the research, lives in Denver. He'll know how to administer the treatment."

Claire: "I can't drive that far with Zoe. She has an appointment tomorrow for PT. Get the doctor to that appointment and I'll give you Mackenzie's location. He brings the cure."

Douglas: "You know it's never been tested on humans before. The doctor was only granted emergency use authorization under the Right to Try law."

Claire: "I'll risk it."

Douglas: "Looks like I'll have to save Mackenzie. She'll keep quiet about this whole affair if Emory gets better, but you'll have to give me everything you were going to use to expose me. The tapes. All of it. And if you ever speak of this, it will be your last day."

Claire: "Agreed."

If only Claire had known that Douglas had arranged for her demise. When Claire had asked to meet the doctor in person, Douglas knew exactly where she'd be. Claire had also assumed the gunman in the park was there for Ashlyn at Douglas's behest.

That was Claire's mistake.

In many respects, Douglas and Claire were cut from the same cloth, and now they were battling it out with innocent lives imprisoned between them. Those two didn't trust each other, and regardless of Claire's motives, she had gone about it the wrong way. Claire had met with the doctor at the appointment. Zoe had been given at least the first dose of a cure. Douglas was going to eliminate any possibility of Claire going to law enforcement and had likely put out a contract on her life. Had Douglas been at the appointment? If he was there, had Claire given him Mackenzie's location?

The tape didn't hold the answer. They were stuck.

As Liam glanced up from the phone, he saw Douglas walking through the entryway to the kitchen, with Ashlyn in front of him. Ashlyn's hands were raised…no doubt a gun pressed to her back.

Douglas had found Ashlyn as she scoured through Claire's bedroom upstairs. Ashlyn had been at Claire's desk, flipping through a day planner, when she found a series of addresses. She'd just picked up the notes to show Liam when she'd smelled a hint of gasoline. As she turned toward the odor, Douglas had come through the door, the weapon pointed directly at her.

"Seems like we had the same thought," Douglas had said.

"I'm here to save someone's life… But it looks like you're here to destroy evidence."

He waved the gun at her. "Downstairs."

Douglas's threatening gestures hadn't drawn a nervous response from Ashlyn. From Liam's assessment, Douglas was inexperienced with weapons, though how could someone miss a shot with the barrel making contact? Could be her training as a nurse had kicked in where, when crisis hit, she could wrestle down the fear and anxiety until the situation was handled. Maybe it was being under the constant threat of danger that had blunted her flight response. She didn't fear Douglas. He operated in the shadows and hired other people to do his misdeeds. His most vicious weapon was seemingly a can of gasoline and a lighter. Though that could do plenty of damage.

Ashlyn had obeyed. If she were going to get any information from Douglas, she'd need Liam's help.

As they'd walked into the kitchen, Liam looked up. He stayed motionless at first, setting the phone back down on the table. He placed his hands on the surface and stood slowly.

"Thought you'd be here," Liam said. "Smells like you're up to arson…again."

Ashlyn looked directly into Liam's eyes. Once they were engaged, she brought her hands forward and pointed them down to the ground. Liam raised an eyebrow and subtly acknowledged her with the faintest nod of his head. With one hand pressed to her chest, she put up one finger, then two, and on three dropped to the ground.

She heard two steps. One on the chair and the other on the kitchen table. The clattering of dishes as they fell and shattered against the worn linoleum floor. A shriek of a cat scurrying away and the tailwind of Liam's body as he flew over her and tackled Douglas. There was a sound of metal clattering, and that was when Ashlyn first risked raising her eyes and saw the gun a few feet away. She scurried toward it on all fours, grabbed it, turned onto her back and raised it. Liam had Douglas facedown on the table, an arm twisted behind his back.

"You good?" Liam asked her.

"I'm good."

Liam pushed his weight into Douglas's back. "Where is she? Where's Mackenzie?"

Douglas met his question with laughter… cold, calculated. The sound of every imagined nightmare rolled up into a heinous expression of what a person normally did when they felt joy.

"It won't matter," Douglas said. "You won't make it in time."

"Find something I can tie him up with," Liam said.

Ashlyn searched her brain with what could be found in a kitchen to accomplish such a task. Her nursing motto kicked in. It didn't have to be fancy…just functional. She scrambled to her feet and set the gun down on the kitchen counter and pulled open several drawers until she found a folded pile of white tea cloths. A few drawers over, she located a pair of kitchen shears. She took two of the towels and nicked through one side with the scissors and tore the towels into strips.

She picked the gun back up and held it at Douglas as she gave Liam the fabric. He made quick work of tying Douglas's hands and feet together. He patted him down, removing the small box of matches from his pocket, and reached for Douglas's phone. He tapped the front and put it in front of Douglas's face so the software would let them in.

"What are you looking for?" Ashlyn asked.

"The contract site." He backed away from

Douglas and motioned Ashlyn over. "I haven't looked at it since we were in Jackson Hole, but if I have access to his phone and account, I can remove the contracts he put out."

He'd found it. There was an account and Ashlyn could see the information, the amount of money, that remained unfulfilled.

"It's not going to matter," Douglas chided. Ashlyn shivered as if her blood were going through a tunnel of ice. What was Douglas talking about? They could see the contract for Ashlyn's life was still active. Liam hit the deactivate button and confirmed. Then he noticed a canceled contract for Mackenzie's life. Good. Everyone should be safe once they found Mackenzie. Liam backtracked through the app and went into active contracts to double-check.

That was when he saw it. A new contract for Mackenzie. Claire had given Douglas Mackenzie's location at the appointment. Which was why she'd made the statements about how little time Mackenzie had left.

Liam nestled the phone to his chest, covering the screen.

"What is it?" Ashlyn asked. "Show me."

Liam looked askance as she plucked the phone from his hands and read through the contract's instructions. Some of the information was encrypted. Maybe once the contract was picked, locations were disguised to prevent someone from getting rescued. There were instructions for a bomb to be placed. It was the most destructive way Douglas could cover up a crime and he'd shown a penchant for wanting things forever splintered. Maybe more than just the crimes he was guilty of. She scrolled up the page and pain zipped along her nerves. Her legs weakened as her vision dimmed.

"Ticktock, ticktock," Douglas said, laughing.

"You can stop this from happening," Liam said to Douglas.

"It's *too* late."

"You should remember that they still have the death penalty in Wyoming. Do you not want to save your own life? Because they're going to find that your fingerprints are all over crimes that have crossed two states."

"Tick…tick…tick…"

Ashlyn's sanity ruptured. Douglas had lost something…just assuming it was his mind would be too much of an understatement. His humanity had dissipated in front of them like a spritz of mist above a blazing fire. She couldn't deal with any more loss in her life. Mackenzie was the one tie she had to who she was. The one person who'd been with her to process her past.

Ashlyn found other active contracts. Several were for bomb placements around the city of

Fort Collins. As she watched, they moved, one by one, to completion. Video attachments were uploading to the account.

As proof.

The last contract listed Mackenzie's name and had her picture next to it. The contract done. The payment processed. In the last fifteen minutes.

There was a video attached.

Liam tugged at the phone. "Let me. You shouldn't watch this."

Ashlyn tightened her grip and stepped away from him to hit Play. It looked like an abandoned school. An old-style blackboard in the background, chipped and crumbling. School desks stacked in the corner. A quick view of the ceiling showed broken tiles with water dripping down. Evidence of the sun melting snow from the recent storm.

Mackenzie, sitting in a room, yelling for help. They had placed something underneath the chair she sat on. Red numbers counting down, but it wasn't clear how much time remained.

"Don't move...don't move," a male voice on the video said.

Those were the last words on the tape.

Liam pulled his weapon and aimed it at Douglas's head. "Give me the address."

"Like you would shoot me."

Liam fired a shot that punctured a round into the floor right next to Douglas's head. "Don't give me a reason."

"If only I believed you, little brother. You'd never kill an innocent. It's against your moral code."

"You're not innocent, though, are you?"

Douglas considered Liam's words. He gave up the address. Liam rifled through his pockets until he found his car keys.

"Where's it parked?" Liam asked.

"Just out front. I needed to be able to escape quickly after my misadventure here."

Ashlyn's lips began to tremble. Something was off about his demeanor—as if he was discarding all his cares away.

As Liam and Ashlyn backed away, Douglas let a strange statement slip from his lips. "You're not going to get far. Just a matter of seconds before the trap I set for you—"

An explosion rocked the upper portion of the house, knocking them both off their feet. Bits of fractured plaster from the ceiling rained down on their heads. A plume of fire arced down the staircase, sparking tertiary fires to the furniture and curtains in its path.

Liam stood and helped Ashlyn up. "Are you hurt?"

Ashlyn wiggled her fingers and toes. No numbness. Everything was moving. "I'm good."

"Go out the back," Liam ordered.

"I'm not leaving without you."

"I'm right behind you. I won't let Douglas die in a fire." Liam reached down and slung Douglas over his shoulder. Once they were a suitable distance from the house, Liam set him in a chair in the rear corner of the backyard. "Hopefully this is a safe place for you to wait until the police pick you up and take you to jail."

# FIFTEEN

Liam put the address into the burner phone. Ten minutes. Ashlyn hopped into the seat next to him and dialed 911, explaining the situation. Liam had the final piece to Douglas's strategy.

Douglas had placed contracts on the dark web for bomb placements. Multiple, cheap contracts. All the contracts required a 911 call except Mackenzie's and would inundate the system. Some contracts didn't require a bomb to be placed. Just a false report called in. The reality of a few actual bombs would place law enforcement on edge, but since some of the calls were turning out to be hoaxes, there wouldn't be a way for them to differentiate between the two unless Liam could provide them a screenshot of the info he had, and the time crunch would not allow that. The most they could hope for was a patrol car to investigate the situation. Most police departments only had one fully trained bomb squad, and those individuals were already playing Douglas's game by trying to find the authentic devices.

Liam replayed the video in his mind. The clock could be a ruse. A component more to terrorize the victim than a countdown to an explosion. The words *Don't move...don't move* ran through Liam's mind like a cheesy song on replay. His stomach knotted. His mind battled the temptation to slip from this moment to something distant. Never did he think he'd be confronted by a situation like this again. An active bomb—a person's life dangling on a cliff's edge. Physically, he was strong enough to do what needed to be done. Mentally, he hoped he could keep it together long enough to take the proper action.

He was speeding. There was little fear of a police officer catching him. Knowing how many serious calls were inundating the system, it could be a criminal free-for-all.

The chaos that Douglas had intentionally created.

Liam took a hard left. His vision grew fuzzy. He reached for Ashlyn's hand. Something, anything, to keep him grounded in this reality. To their right, they could see the fractured playground. Chunks of old asphalt upturned. Nylon basketball nets frayed by wind and cold. The remaining metal hoops bent by the weight of hundreds of kids playing fanciful basketball in their mind. Several windows were broken. Long-faded paint in various primary colors marking the playground for games of hopscotch and four square. Liam tore into the parking lot and threw the car into Park, their seat belts restraining them from being ejected through the windshield.

They exited the car. Liam faced Ashlyn.

"What are you waiting for?" Ashlyn said.

"You're not going in with me."

She pushed past him and walked toward the entrance. "You don't have a choice in the matter."

He grabbed her arm and pulled her back. Gently, he eased her against the hood of the car. "I don't want you in there. You won't do me any good. You're better off out here waiting for the police. They'll need someone to explain what's going on. Show the officer the information on Douglas's phone. It will help them see Mackenzie is the one at risk. Hopefully, they'll shift their resources here. Tell them not to come into the building without a bomb specialist."

"I'm not staying here."

"*You will* because that's the best option. If this doesn't go the right way…you're the only one to care for Emory." Liam inhaled deeply. "After this, we're over."

Ashlyn's eyes widened and glimmered as tears built up in the corners.

He forced himself to continue. Made himself say anything that would cement her feet to the ground where she stood. He wouldn't risk her life. He'd rather live without her than face her death.

"You're not the right person for me."

Ashlyn slumped against the vehicle. "You… don't mean it."

He drew closer to her and locked her eyes with his. "I mean every word. Ever since you came into my life… I've wanted to help you solve what happened to Mackenzie, but I want my life to go back to the way it was. Whatever happens today…it is the end of us."

Liam straightened his shoulders and walked two steps backward. She buried her face in her hands and he turned and walked into the building.

He drew the weapon from his side. His feet felt like lead. His heart had shattered, and the shards cut open his insides. His chest zinged with pain. It was something he'd never felt before. The utter disconnect between telling a lie and wanting to live with the truth.

Liam squared his stance. He had to silo his feelings for the moment to deal with the task at hand. The heavy metal school doors were open to one side. He slid through the entrance. He couldn't bear a backward glance toward Ashlyn. Seeing the state she was in would make it impossible to complete what he needed to do. All he'd want to do would be to take her in his arms and ease her suffering. Those were the right things to say, but not for her benefit…for his. There wasn't a way he could see, the way his life was now, being emotionally available to her in the way she needed. She'd need so much more than he could give.

Ultimately, though the words stung, for her it would be better than the life sentence of dealing with him and his issues.

Liam looked down at the dusty floor. The advantage for law enforcement in dealing with bombs in an abandoned building was the fine layer of dust that lay on the ground, which made it easy to see the criminal's footprints in the sheen of light.

He stepped slowly along the path left by these prints. Glancing side to side. Listening for any noise. The footprints turned in a room up ahead and Liam went inside.

Mackenzie was there, poised in the middle of the room. There was duct tape over her mouth. They'd tied her from behind. Liam holstered his weapon and raised his hands in the air, assuming as much of a nonthreatening pose as he could.

"I'm Liam. I'm a friend of Ashlyn's. I'm here to help but stay sitting still."

She nodded. The countdown clock sat on a table next to her. It was at thirty seconds and moving quickly.

Liam approached the device. He traced the wires to the central explosive. A bundle of C-4 taped underneath the seat.

Fifteen seconds.

After a quick examination of the device, he stood.

"It's going to be okay." He gently removed the tape from her mouth.

Five seconds.

"You need to go!" she yelled.

He put a hand on top of the device and rested a firm hand on her shoulder.

"You and I are both walking out of here. Just don't move one inch." He prayed what he was saying was true.

Two...one...

They both reflexively closed their eyes, expecting the worst. Liam held his breath for a solid five seconds before he dared open an eye.

"Stay still," he ordered.

He looked at Mackenzie. Tears were coursing down her face. He stroked her upper back. "We're not out of the woods yet. You're sitting on a pressure-sensitive plate. If you move to get up, that's what will set the device off."

"Is Emory safe?"

"She is back in Jackson Hole with a good friend of mine. Under his protection."

She nodded, understanding. "Where's Ashlyn?"

"She's waiting for you outside."

"What's your plan? Why aren't the police here?"

Liam settled on his haunches and reexamined the device. Looking into Mackenzie's terror-filled eyes was a direct connection with the eyes of those children he hadn't been able to save. Today, there was no one present who could deter him from his mission. The culmination of what he hadn't accomplished then was the task that faced him now.

Was this God? Was it Liam's destiny? Would this act, whether he lived or died, be the way he achieved forgiveness for failing those children before?

He didn't wish for death but was comfortable if that was the outcome. If it saved Ashlyn and Mackenzie. If it gave Emory back to her mother. If it saved the world from any further actions his brother would ever take, then it would be worth it in the end.

Liam crawled to the other side of the chair. There was nothing pinning Mackenzie to it. She could have gotten up at any point and it would have been the death of her. Having the fortitude to stay put when everything in her body told her otherwise was a strength he'd seen in few people.

"Did you know Douglas was so evil?"

It was her posing the question to him. He settled on the floor and scooted under the chair slightly. The bomb was more complex than he'd anticipated. That was when he saw the note taped there with his name on it. They'd attached the note to the chair separate from the device and he gently pulled it away. He didn't have the faith in himself to determine which wires to cut to deactivate it. That left only one alternative. He wiggled himself slowly on the ground away from the chair and stood up. He was behind Mackenzie when he opened the note.

*Take her place.*

Liam contemplated the meaning of the note. If Douglas had designed this contract, Liam had to dive into his psyche to determine the note's meaning.

"I could ask you the same thing," Liam responded, if anything to keep Mackenzie engaged in a conversation, keep her still, and give him more time to discern what the note meant.

He knew that the longer he took to settle on his choice, the more risk there was that Ashlyn would decide she couldn't stay outside the building anymore. Doing nothing was not an option in her mindset. Especially if people she loved were at risk. Telling a critical-care nurse to stand by and do nothing when there was a crisis at hand was only going to give him a few minutes.

Mackenzie licked her dry lips. "There's a difference between mean and evil. Douglas has crossed over that line. I can't say exactly when it happened. Maybe I've known that he flirted with those edges for a while. I guess much could be said about me…about how I manipulated the situation with him to get what I wanted."

Liam shifted back to take a broad look at the scene in front of him. "You didn't make the best choices, either, but you were trying to save your child. I don't think you would have gone public with the affair because him not achieving his political goals would have meant less money in going after the cure for Emory."

Mackenzie looked down, shame like a yoke across her shoulders.

"Emory's lucky to have a mother like you. Willing to fight for the things she needs. The rest…as they say…is between you and God."

Mackenzie raised her eyes to him. "Thank you…for not making me feel worse than I already do."

Maybe the clock had more meaning than what he gave it. "Have you seen the clock count down more than once?"

"No…just the one time."

"How much time was there on it before?" Liam honestly didn't know if it would have any meaning.

"One hour."

"And you're sitting on some type of plate?"

"Yes—it's why I haven't moved an inch since I was brought here."

Liam had to give Douglas credit. He hadn't thought he was devious enough to weave a web this tight. It was theorized that politicians had the characteristics of a psychopath—they just didn't murder people. Those qualities were essential to the job that they had to do. The lying. The deceit. Douglas's environmental training during his youth—the abuse and abandonment— would have watered the seeds of whatever he'd been born with to make his psychopathic tendencies grow. After receiving Mackenzie's location, Douglas had provided it to potential bomb makers, but the note really meant the ultimate destruction was meant for him.

For Liam.

With perhaps Mackenzie as collateral damage.

The last time Liam had visited Douglas, he'd asked him about Liam's weight.

"Here's the plan." Liam rounded to the back of the chair, took a knife from his pocket and cut through the zip ties. Mackenzie rubbed her thumbs over the raw, reddened skin. Zip ties placed to her wrists over the last hour wouldn't have done that much damage. She'd been tied up for days—the skin deterioration was evidence of how tight her ligatures had been and how much she'd struggled against them.

"You're going to get up and run out of here. Ashlyn is out front. Hopefully the police are out there, and the bomb squad is waiting to come in."

"You don't think it will blow up as soon as I stand up?"

He knelt in front of her. "I don't know, but I think they made this trap for me and not you." He showed her the note. "I'm to take your place."

Mackenzie cried. She pressed her face into her hands to control her sobbing, but her body shook regardless. Liam settled his hands on her shoulders. "Shh…please, don't cry so hard. It's going to be okay."

"I couldn't forgive myself. Ashlyn would never forgive me if you died. I'll just stay here until the bomb squad gets here. They'll know the way to get me out of this."

There was a loud, piercing beep in the room. Liam and Mackenzie brought their hands over their ears to muffle the sound.

"The clock!" Mackenzie yelled.

Liam turned to look. It was counting down… ten seconds. Liam, praying he was right about all his assumptions, yanked Mackenzie off the chair.

"Run!" he told her and shoved her toward the exit of the classroom. She did as he instructed.

Liam first tried to put pressure on the plate to see if it would stop the countdown. It didn't change the downward trajectory of the numbers.

He couldn't clear the distance to the exit. Mackenzie wasn't far enough away to leave the building uninjured.

Three…two…

Liam turned and sat down.

The numbers reset to thirty minutes.

This time Liam knew that if someone didn't help things change course, this bomb was going to detonate in thirty minutes.

Ashlyn couldn't take it anymore. Liam's words had stung, but regardless of whether he wanted to end things or not, she would not let him die alone. She had to see Mackenzie one more time, and if that meant the demise of all three…she was at peace with it.

She pushed away from the car and began marching toward the building when Mackenzie ran through the front door. Ashlyn stopped in her tracks, overwhelmed with emotion, and her legs buckled. Mackenzie swallowed her up in a bear hug. Ashlyn wept. The sound of a siren pealed through the air as an officer turned sharply into the parking lot.

"Where's Liam?" Ashlyn asked her sister.

"He's inside."

"Is he safe?"

All Mackenzie could do was shake her head. Ashlyn pushed past her to go inside the building, but Mackenzie grabbed her arm to hold her back. "You can't."

The officer approached them, and her sister ran right for him. "There's a bomb in the building. A man—he's trapped on top of it." Mackenzie waved her hands in front of her body as if the motion would bring forth the words she was trying to say. "He's sitting on…some sort of… pressure plate. But the clock, it must be counting down again."

The officer spoke into the radio, calling for a bomb team to his location. "Do you know how much time?"

"When I ran, there were seconds on the timer, so it must have reset. I don't know how much time is left."

The officer heard words come back through the radio. "Seems your friend is on the phone with 911 asking for some help from the ordnance team." He put his finger in the air. "Caller confirms the clock is counting down from thirty minutes. Bomb team is about ten minutes out. We've had a slew of false reports and some fake bombs planted around the area. Seems like what your friend is sitting on could be the real deal."

"I'm sorry," Mackenzie said to Ashlyn. "He pulled me off the device. They timed it to restart after so many minutes and there was this note…"

Ashlyn pulled Mackenzie closer to her. "I don't blame you. I'm glad we found you. Emory will have her mother back."

"If Liam doesn't live…you'll never forgive me."

Ashlyn contemplated the question. "There will be nothing to forgive. Liam did what he thought was right in the moment."

She was trying to be brave for Mackenzie, but Ashlyn's world was crashing in on her. The tension in her body made her feel like her cells were ripping apart. Like she would evaporate, at any moment, from the pressure. She wanted to scream. To run and hit something. She wanted to drift away. Pinch herself to wake up.

Liam had said he didn't want to be with her. That would be hard enough to accept. His death…she didn't know if she'd have the strength to go on.

# SIXTEEN

Liam sat there, watching the moments of his life tick away. Twenty minutes remained. *Will I feel anything? Did those little girls in Afghanistan feel anything?* He felt unusually calm considering his circumstances. Normal pulse rate and breathing. Was this what a life review felt like? He was in that zone where, though he was close to death…his mind was clear. Thoughts crystallized when the mind wasn't distracted by other things because mortality and its meaning became transparent and ever-pressing.

It was the idea of substitution and what it meant that was plaguing Liam. He'd read the Bible when he was overseas and understood the tenets of believing in a God who had laid down His life so others could have something that could otherwise not be given if they just believed in what He had done.

This was the first time it ever seemed personal to him.

The sky darkened. Through the dirty, broken windows, snow fell in fat, wet flakes. It hit the out-facing glass of the classroom and created sluices of clear rivulets as it melted down the dusty panes—like tears.

This was what Ashlyn had been trying to say. That Jesus first came as a child, but ultimately became a sacrifice. And through that action became the fulfillment of what many thought could never be obtained again. Unity. Mercy. Grace.

Peace.

Taking Mackenzie's place hadn't been a hard decision to make. Of course, he didn't want to take it through to its conclusion. He hoped against the odds that the bomb squad could fix the ordeal that he'd put himself in.

Ashlyn had said sometimes God takes drastic action when He's trying to garner the attention of lost people.

Liam rubbed his hands over his knees. Before Ashlyn had shared her thoughts on what Christmas meant to her, it hadn't been real to him. If he'd been in this situation before he'd met Ashlyn, he would have deemed his circumstances a consequential action of what had happened overseas. A universal payback for his failure. Of course he should die in the same way those children had perished when he could not help them.

Now maybe this was the wake-up call he

needed. This substitution brought life to others. His sacrifice meant Emory would have a mother. Even if he couldn't be saved, he now knew he would be okay in the end, regardless of the outcome.

In that moment, two bomb squad members came through the door.

One approached, and the other hung back. Walking in bomb squad gear was a slow, lumbering process. "Looks like you've got yourself in quite a pickle here."

The man eyed the clock with its ten minutes ticking down and got down on all fours and looked under Liam's chair. "I don't think whoever set this wanted you to make it out alive."

"I gathered that."

"I'm not sure we'll have the time to examine the mechanics enough in ten minutes to get you off this thing."

"It's okay… I understand. You can leave me."

"Oh no. We're not leaving you. That's why I've got this on. Question is—how do we protect you when the bomb detonates, because it looks like that's the scenario we'll have to deal with."

"I don't want you to put yourself in harm's way."

The man placed an assuring hand on Liam's shoulder. "I'm here for you today. We're leaving this building together. Understood?"

It was the first time Liam had felt genuine hope in a very long time.

The shock wave threw Ashlyn onto her back. The first thing she registered was the oddity of the blue sky and the column of black smoke roiling over her vision. The building crackled like popcorn bursting. Acrid smoke filled her nostrils, and a cough signaled her lungs were forcefully trying to prevent the soot from entering. She turned onto her side to see Mackenzie sitting up and facing her.

Mackenzie placed a hand on her cheek and mouthed, "I'm sorry."

Ashlyn sat up. Within a few minutes of the bomb squad arriving, the fire department had been on-site and now were running hoses up to the building. Though they were fighting back emotion, Ashlyn could tell from the body language of the bomb squad they feared the worst. Two had their backs turned from the building. One had his thumb and index finger pressed against his eyes.

The world opened underneath Ashlyn. A black, smoky sky. A dark well of despair sucked her down into the void. Her mind couldn't process the calamity in front of her. The various departments shouting orders to one another. The radio traffic trying to raise a response from the team members who had gone inside after Liam. Her heart was a stone weight inside her chest. She couldn't breathe. Mackenzie's voice was a thousand miles away. Her ears were ringing.

*Please, God. Let those men be okay. Bring them out of this fire. Let Liam be alive.*

"We're here." A static crackle through the radios.

A blanket of silence covered their mouths. Ears perked for verification.

"Repeat," an officer demanded through his comms.

"We're coming out. All of us."

Through the doors came Liam, sandwiched between two bomb squad members. Ashlyn ran toward him and collapsed into him, her tears mixing with the soot that covered his body, creating a black smudge that muddied her face. She gripped his jacket, pulling him close, and looked up into his eyes, only to be met by a vacant stare. Eventually, he looked down and she could not discern what his mind was thinking.

"You're not safe here," Liam said.

At the same moment, an officer approached her and Mackenzie. "We're going to take you two to the police station for statements. Hopefully, ma'am, we'll be able to get you back to Jackson Hole today to be reunited with your little girl."

"You need to go," Liam instructed.

Ashlyn dropped her hands to her sides. There were so many things she wanted to do in this moment. Tell him he was wrong. Fight for them to be together. Say that they could work through whatever doubts he had about them being together…about them being a family. But the look in his eyes told her he wasn't open to any such discussion. He was resigned. There wasn't a spark of feistiness left.

She turned away and followed the officer— leaving behind all she hoped she and Liam would be.

# SEVENTEEN

The evening had been a blur. Police interviews. Written statements. Douglas under arrest. Claire in the hospital…unknown if she would survive or not. The crimes that Douglas was being investigated for were mind-numbingly impressive. He'd accomplished more as a criminal than he ever had as a politician. What he'd be known for would be far different from the legacy he had dreamed of. He was in the running for most disgraced politician instead of loving father and philanthropist—those costumes falling away from his facade like cheap material. Ashlyn was aware of Liam's presence at the police station. For several hours, she'd been sitting alone in an interrogation room so her statement to police wouldn't be influenced by others and the events they'd witnessed. To ferret out if her claimed innocence was the truth or just another part of the nefarious plot that Douglas had woven.

When she and Mackenzie were reunited, they

were taken to the airport, where a flight would take them back to Jackson Hole.

"What am I going to do?" Mackenzie asked.

"In what sense?"

"With Emory. I don't have a home to go back to. No job. How will I care for her?"

Ashlyn turned. "We have each other. We always will. You can come live with me."

Mackenzie scoffed. "Two people and an infant smashed together in your tiny studio apartment. How will you work nights and be able to sleep during the day with a baby in your home?"

Ashlyn looked out of the window. The perspective from up above the clouds calmed her. The light fluffiness levitated her mood. She forced herself to count her blessings. She and Mackenzie were alive. Emory was well. Soon they would be reunited. Even if she and Liam weren't meant to be together, he had made it through the ordeal and hopefully would come to terms with all that had happened and be in connection with people and not lead an isolated life anymore. It hurt beyond measure he had pushed her away, and she tried to reason that his feelings were momentary. That almost losing his life would have changed the trajectory he'd set—one of choosing to isolate himself more. Unfortunately, there was nothing she could do about his choices, and she wasn't the type of woman to grovel for any man. She wanted him to be whole...to have a fulfilled life, and she hoped that someday they could have that together.

But if he chose not to, then there was little she could do to change his mind.

"I've been thinking about Claire's child," Ashlyn said.

"I know. I have been, too."

"Why didn't you tell me about Claire? About her daughter?" Ashlyn asked.

"I was scared. I was...selfish. I had shared about the possibility of Emory's illness before she even told me she had a daughter. Once I found out how sick Zoe was, I was so scared there wouldn't be enough of the cure for Emory if her child was treated."

"We don't even know what symptoms Emory will have," Ashlyn said.

"I know. Thanks for making me feel worse. I guess we'll find out if the mRNA vaccine the doctor produced will induce Zoe's body to make the protein it needs for muscle function."

"In a way, it's probably better for Emory. You'll know if the cure really works. In the same instance, it's so dangerous for Zoe to be given something experimental. It's not been studied or peer-reviewed."

"It's not making me feel any better about the

decisions I made. I don't know how you do it, Ashlyn. Make the choices you do in nursing."

"Mackenzie, I'm not judging. I don't know what I would do if I had a child that was sick with only one dose of a cure available. It's easy to pass judgment on others when you've never been in the situation yourself."

They were silent for several minutes. Ashlyn knew once she spoke the next words there would be little she could do to take them back. It would be a pledge she would have to live up to.

"I'm going to petition the courts to be guardian over Zoe in case Claire doesn't survive," Ashlyn said.

"How will you take care of her? You don't have the money. You'll need help."

"I'll find a way. I am a nurse, after all. A pediatric one at that."

"The money it takes… You'd have to quit your job to provide her care. You can barely afford the apartment you live in. The court will never allow it."

It perturbed Ashlyn that Mackenzie wasn't being more supportive of this idea. After all she'd risked just to bring her sister back alive.

Would Ashlyn do differently? She'd probably try to reason with Mackenzie, too, if she shot out such a harebrained idea.

"I'm Zoe's aunt, though, right? I have an obligation to care for family."

Mackenzie's face paled. Ashlyn's stomach lurched. There was a mask of dread people wore when they didn't want to share what was on their mind. Tight, pressed lips. The averted glance. Ashlyn's legs felt heavy. All the blood had pooled there.

"You and I," Mackenzie started, "are not biologically related."

If Ashlyn could have run away, she would have. If there had been a parachute on the plane, she would have strapped it on, opened the door and leaped with abandon. Her life as she had known it, the truths she had counted on, had vanished in one day.

She didn't have a family…none.

"How long have you known?" Ashlyn's voice was tight. The words were high and squeaky. She was having difficulty taking a deep breath.

Mackenzie exhaled and fisted her hands. "A while. When I had the genetic testing done, I stole one of your toothbrushes. I wanted to know if you were a carrier, and you were refusing to get tested. You wanted children so badly and I knew in my heart you couldn't face it if you came up having the disease. There wasn't any chance you would risk passing on something like this to any offspring. That's when I found out we weren't related."

"But I remember growing up with you. I remember our mother…"

"I remember you coming to live with us. You were just an infant. Mom, from the get-go, offered no explanation as to your arrival. She just called you my sister, and that's what you became. Then Claire sort of vanished and it was just the two of us. Then she couldn't care for us, and we ended up in foster care."

Nothing Ashlyn knew was real anymore.

Mackenzie gripped her hand. "We will always be sisters. No matter how you came into my family…you are my family. My only family. Nothing is going to change that. At least, nothing will change it in my mind, and I hope it doesn't change in your mind, either. Don't let something like this tear you away from me. You're Emory's aunt. You're the only family she will have… Don't take yourself away from us. Families are not just based on biological ties and genetic material."

Ashlyn's throat was thick. The grief in her mind overwhelmed any cogent thought. She couldn't claim anyone as her own.

Everything that had anchored her in her life had been clipped free and she was trying to stand upright in hurricane-force winds.

\* \* \*

Liam sat on his couch, looking at the tree that Ashlyn had created for them. In front of him was the entire scope of letters that Ashlyn had written to him over the last three years. Where he usually kept a weapon, those letters had now taken its place. Two letters a month. Cards for most holidays. Photos. He'd just finished reading each one.

It was unbearably quiet in the cabin. A few weeks had passed since his adventure with Ashlyn. Usually, the solace was comforting. Now it was unnerving. He missed hearing Emory's peals of laughter. It was as if the explosion had punched through his gut and what remained was a hole that threatened to consume him. *Regret* was too mild a word for what he was feeling. He'd done it…successfully pushed Ashlyn away. And what he thought he wanted in life…isolation and protection…now his body couldn't tolerate. He longed to have her back in his arms. To hold her. To feel the softness of her skin under his touch. To talk with her about all the things they talked about.

He wanted to take back everything he'd said to her at the school. To tell her every word had been a lie. That he didn't believe any of it.

He didn't want to live this life anymore. He wanted to be with her. He wanted to give her the family she wanted.

He wanted to be her family.

There was a knock at the door. Liam scrambled to his feet and stumbled as he ran to it. Throwing it open, he saw Doc standing there, blowing out puffs of crystallized air as he exhaled.

Liam's shoulders sagged as he stepped aside.

"Thanks for the warm welcome," Doc said. He came through the entranceway on crutches. Liam glanced out. The car that had dropped him off was driving away. Looked like Doc intended to stay for a while.

"Sorry," Liam offered.

"No trouble. I'm guessing you were hoping I was someone else."

Liam helped Doc get seated, took his pair of crutches and leaned them against the leather couch.

"How is Ashlyn? And everyone?"

Doc chuckled. "It's a full house right now, with Ashlyn, Mackenzie and Emory. We celebrated a late Christmas and New Year's. I am loving every moment. Makes my heart feel warm to have them there." Doc leaned forward and grabbed one of Ashlyn's letters. "Seems like you've been taking a trip down memory lane."

Liam sat next to him. "You didn't answer my question."

Doc set the letter gently back on top of the

pile. "A long time ago I told you I would never lie to you, so I might as well keep that promise. You broke her heart, Liam. Ashlyn puts on a brave face. Because of the lack of medical foster homes…well, everywhere… Zoe's living with us, too. Since Mackenzie is biologically Zoe's aunt, the court granted Mackenzie temporary custody in the wake of Claire's death, but Ashlyn feels she is to care for Zoe, considering her background and experience. Mackenzie doesn't appear to want that kind of long-term responsibility."

"That doesn't surprise me," Liam said.

It had been two weeks since the events in Fort Collins. Douglas remained in jail without the benefit of bail. Colorado and Wyoming were fighting over who would try him first. The level of criminality that Douglas exhibited in Colorado could rise to a death penalty case, but Colorado had abolished those laws. Regardless of the court's decision, Douglas would likely be in prison the rest of his life but would live. The news would feed off this story for the next decade.

"Why did you do it? Push her away so mercilessly?" Doc asked.

"I was afraid of…hurting her."

Doc patted Liam's thigh. "It's not something you have in you, Liam. I know with your PTSD you believe you could mistake her for an enemy and cause harm to her. You've been in some of the most intense situations in the past month since you left the military, and you did nothing but protect her. Want to give me the genuine answer?"

"Fear...that I couldn't ever be what she wanted."

"But instead of trying, you ended up fulfilling your worst fear anyway. Here you are... alone. Staring at the same four walls you've jailed yourself in for the last year."

"I know... I've been thinking a lot about that. I used to never live this way. I was willing to take on any challenge. I used to love...being around people. The military was the family I never had growing up. But when I lost...friends and...those children... I just got to a point where I didn't want to handle loss anymore."

"And yet you are dealing with loss every day here." Doc placed a hand on his shoulder. "This journey of life, it's not an easy one. There will always be losses. Friends and family are the bright spots that God gives us to better weather those losses when they happen. Of course, those are also some of the most painful losses we'll ever have. A spouse dying. A child dying before we do. I dread the day Dolores leaves this earth. Hopefully, I'll die before her. The grief would be that terrible for me." Doc dropped his arm and folded his hands in his lap. "That despair will be worth every moment I was given to spend with her. It's worth that look between two people that other people don't understand. That…heart-to-heart connection you only have with one other person. I think God gives us that as just a tiny glimmer of what heaven will be like. Something to sustain us through the mire we're living in down here. Liam, my friend, you'll be living every day like Ashlyn died when you could spend innumerable days together and have more joy in your life than you ever thought possible."

It was a knife to his heart. Doc was right. He would live with this pain and loneliness all his days if he didn't change it. In pushing Ashlyn away, he'd given himself a life sentence when he had the freedom to do otherwise. Was he really choosing to live like Douglas when he had done no such crime? Was he choosing to give up the freedom that he'd spilled his own blood for overseas? If he was, he was dishonoring everything he believed in. He was mocking what he'd picked up a weapon for. He, above anyone, fully realized what living in freedom meant, and he wasn't taking advantage of it. Tears trickled down his face, and he wiped them away.

"I don't want to live like this."

Doc shifted and opened the jacket he'd been wearing. "Ashlyn wanted me to give you these.

She came here earlier, was going to give them to you in person, but you weren't here, and she said she couldn't take coming back again."

He handed Liam two envelopes, which Liam tucked into his back pocket to read later.

After spending a bit more time with Liam, Doc grabbed his crutches and stood, Liam helping him to the door. When he opened it, he saw Dolores waiting for him at the base of the stairs.

She waved and Liam helped to get Doc settled in the car.

"If you want Ashlyn back, you know what you need to do."

Liam closed the door and walked back into the cabin. He pulled the notes from his pocket. The one he opened first had been in Emory's carrier when Ashlyn had left her on his doorstep.

*Liam,*
*I know this letter is strange, but I'm in trouble. This is my niece, Emory. I'm leaving her with you for protection. I believe my sister has been murdered and I'm going to find who her killer is. I know that we have never met, but after all these years of writing letters to you, you're the only man I trust to do this...take care of the last thing in this world that is precious to me. I've*

*hoped for a long time that we would meet in person. That I could meet the person who has been such an enormous influence on my life. Your letters are one of the few things that kept me going through these last years. I didn't realize what a lonely life I'd been living until I wrote to you, and I just wanted you to know, if we never meet, how much that meant to me and I thank you for being the man that you are. You probably feel like I was your lifeline...but really, you were mine.*
*Ashlyn*

He placed the note carefully in its envelope and placed it on top of the stack he'd been reading through. Picking up the last note, he held it in his hands. Would this be the last thing Ashlyn would ever write to him? Could he win her back?

*Liam,*
*It's strange to be writing these words on paper when I wanted to tell them to you in person. I stopped by yesterday and you weren't home. I didn't have the heart to come back, but I still wanted to say these words to you. Maybe putting pen to paper is good because then you'll always have*

*them. The only thing you'll be missing is the depth of emotion that comes with them. The look in my eyes. The feel of my touch against your face. The force of meaning in my words.*

*We spent a harrowing week together. Most of it running from danger, granted. They say a person's worst qualities are revealed under pressure. The stress of the event takes away all normal coping mechanisms. The essence of a person emerges when their facade is stripped down while they're in a pressure cooker.*

*What became clear to me is the person you really are. The difference between you and your brother is striking. Douglas was laid bare down to his true evil nature. You, Liam, were a light in the darkness. You stayed with me. Comforted me. Gave me safety and security. I never thought you would leave me. I wasn't disposable to you the way I had been to so many people before.*

*I'm learning more now about what the definition of family really means. I found out that Mackenzie and I are not biologically related. Why would she want to continue to call me her sister when she doesn't need to? Then I realized we're all adopted into the most important family we can have. We are not biologically God's children, but we get adopted into His family when we believe. We're in His family by choice. Mackenzie is every part my sister now, maybe more so, because she chooses me, and that decision is unwavering.*

*I love you, Liam. Without you, I feel lost. I feel like a part of me is missing. I feel like my family is not complete. I understand the choice you made and am trying to respect your space and live with it, but I pray every day that something in your heart will change. I hope you find what you're looking for. I hope you find peace, but ultimately, I hope you find someone to love…even if it isn't me.*
*Ashlyn*

Liam folded the letter. The next thing he did was pull a card from his wallet and dial the number. "I need to make an appointment. I'm having trouble with… PTSD. I want to get better."

# EIGHTEEN

Ashlyn and Mackenzie were back in court. Ashlyn was attempting to get custody of Claire's daughter, Zoe. Her mind was tumultuous with thoughts of Liam and the letters Doc had delivered one week ago. Hoping the notes would light a fire under Liam and spur him to reach out hadn't come to fruition.

"Miss Sutton." The judge's voice focused her attention to the bench. "I appreciate your exuberance over wanting to take over the care of Zoe, and the help you've provided to Mackenzie is nothing less than honorable. Unfortunately, in your current state, I can't grant you custody."

"I have secure employment, Your Honor. I've given up my primary residence. The couple I'm staying with has ample room. The environment is stable."

"All those are good points, but this man's generosity is not a long-term solution. Being gainfully employed is a plus, but you haven't been able to secure replacement medical services for Zoe while you're working and, by the social worker's report, your sister hasn't proved to be an adequate replacement for your care. Mackenzie is relying on a… Dolores Montgomery to do most of the care while you're away. I don't fault you, Mackenzie. I'd rather you not put yourself in a situation you can't handle long term. From the submitted medical reports, your own child is at risk of suffering some of these same effects, and caring for two children with a myriad of medical complications is clearly more than the court should ask you to bear."

"What do I need to do, then, Your Honor, for you to grant me custody?" Ashlyn asked.

"Zoe, though improving, requires round-the-clock medical care like she was getting in her previous state of residence. Though it pains me to say, this child was probably better off in Colorado. I'm not sure we have enough people with the specialized pediatric nursing care here in our smaller, less metropolitan city—particularly with the nursing shortage across the nation."

"I'm a pediatric nurse."

"I'm aware of your qualifications. I'm not saying you're not trained. I'm saying you're between a rock and a hard place. You need money to take care of Zoe. To get that money, you need a job, but that very job also takes the one person away that would qualify you for custody. Unless, of course, you can find in-home help that the state cannot provide."

"What's the answer, then?" Ashlyn asked, tears threatening to fall.

"I know you're in a frustrating place and I fully admire what you're trying to accomplish. I've outlined for you what it will take for you to achieve custody. Considering your tenacity, I have no doubt you'll come up with some creative solutions. When that happens, you can petition the court again, but I also need to consider the welfare of the child. If you can't achieve these things over the next three months by your next check-in with social services, the court will have to consider placing the child into a medical foster care so I can be sure her needs are met."

"I'm her family. There would be no reason to place her into foster care."

"Technically, Mackenzie here is her biological family, but considering the unusualness of the situation, I'm working with all of you for the benefit of this child. You'll find a way, Ashlyn. I know." The judge tapped his gavel. "Court is adjourned."

Liam felt more nervous today than the day he'd first entered his bedroom and seen Ashlyn disheveled with a cut to her forehead, pine needles scattered in her hair and a laceration to her head from a gunshot wound. The air was brisk. Winter had fully settled in. It would be a while before the snow melted enough to see grass and spring flowers.

His heart rammed against his ribs like a rabbit running away from a predator. He waited at the base of the courthouse steps, light-headed, anticipating her arrival. Gripping the cold steel of the handrail, expecting his flesh would freeze to it to keep him in place. The outer door to the courthouse pushed open and Mackenzie emerged first with their lawyer. Ashlyn walked a few steps behind, her face downcast. Mackenzie caught sight of him first and halted her steps, causing Ashlyn to bump into her backside. When Ashlyn's eyes lifted, he looked at her helplessly and waved. After a few words between the sisters, Mackenzie and the lawyer peeled off and Ashlyn stepped slowly down the stairs like a reluctant bride heading to the altar.

Could he blame her? His last words to her had been like acid to flesh. Did the scars of that conversation remain? By her look, they ran deep.

Ashlyn stopped two stairs above him, perhaps unconsciously taking the higher ground.

Liam shoved his hands in his pockets and bit his lips. These first words would likely determine if her feet stayed planted or if she followed her sister to the car.

"I've missed you," Liam said.

He saw her inhale sharply. When he engaged her eyes, they glistened, the wells of her eyes filling with tears.

"How are you?" Ashlyn asked.

A hollow opened in his chest and fear seeped in. This wasn't the reaction he'd hoped for. Hearing an *I miss you back* would have been a salve to his wounds, but he wasn't here for his own sake. Or was he? He had ground to make up.

"I was at the court hearing. I'm...sorry... things didn't go your way."

Ashlyn took hold of the rail and took one more step down. "I'm not sure they will. I don't know how to meet the judge's demands without help and I can't depend on Doc to keep us indefinitely. He deserves a calm life with Dolores. Not caring for a constellation of people that he doesn't owe anything to."

Liam chuckled nervously. "He would probably disagree with you there. He loves having you there. I don't know that he would want it any different."

"Do you want things to be different?" Ashlyn asked, her eyes boring into his. "Why are you here today?"

"I just...wanted to check in on you. Your letters...meant everything." The tips of his fingers tingled. His heart stalled. "I'm sorry for the things I said at the school. I wish I could be different. I wish I could be the man you wanted me to be. I want to help, but I don't think I can... risk it."

"Am I to take your apology to mean you were mistaken when you said I wasn't the right person for you?" There was a tinge of hope in her voice.

Liam swallowed hard. "You are the right person for me, but *I'm not* the right person for you." Sharp pains flittered through his chest like a knife probing. He couldn't bear to look at her, but he forced himself to. It was an ideal from the military—sharing in one another's burdens, even if it caused a permanent wound to the psyche. She took the last step down. Her disappointment settled into his soul like a cancer. It would live with him unless he did something about it. Sought out some sort of cure. According to his new therapist, self-inflicted wounds could be healed.

Ashlyn unzipped his jacket and unbuttoned the top of his shirt, sliding her hand underneath and pressing it over his heart. She looked up into his eyes. "I want you to see the man that I see. This whole adventure we survived together has been a redemption for you, Liam. Evidence that all the things you think about yourself aren't true. Zoe and Emory are alive today because you helped me when you could have done the easy thing and turned your back. You never hurt me—all you did was protect me. You're not broken…any more than the rest of us. I just wish…you could love me the way I love you." She pulled her hand away and all he wanted to do was grip it and hold her close.

"I want that, too. Maybe someday…"

Ashlyn shoved her hands into her coat. The same white coat he'd found her in. It was cleaned and the torn fabric stitched closed by her hand. Her inability to buy a new one spoke volumes. She was likely using every spare dime to care for Zoe.

Seeing that split something within him.

"I think you, of all people, know this, Liam. We're not guaranteed tomorrow. Wishing for someday is giving up on a lot of life you could be living today."

An echo of Doc's words. Was God trying to get his attention? If so, it was high time he started listening.

What could he do to be the man that she needed?

# NINETEEN

It was a week since Ashlyn had seen Liam at the courthouse steps. Mackenzie told her she was foolish to keep holding out hope that Liam would change. Each day that went by, her optimism dimmed a little more. Had he meant to finally push her away? That someday would never happen. Her mind couldn't convince her heart to believe it.

Every day since then, she'd obsessively checked the mail for a letter. Sometimes standing by Doc's mailbox waiting for the postman to come. She'd ask anyone who'd run errands in town if they'd seen Liam. If so, had he had anything for her? The sightings had been rare—not unusual for the town hero. Ashlyn figured it wasn't unexpected, considering the press coverage of Douglas's crimes, but surely the man had to buy a few provisions now and then? Had he returned to the sheltered life he'd lived before? Hadn't her words changed anything?

On a day when Ashlyn was sitting next to the mailbox waiting again for delivery, a large white van pulled up in front of Doc's house.

To her surprise, Liam exited, walked up to her and held out his hand. "I was wondering if you were available for a trip to the cabin?"

Ashlyn stood. Hesitation spread through her body. Was she ready for what this could be? "I might be, but…"

Liam took her hand and turned her toward Doc's compound. Doc stood there at the window with Dolores and Zoe, a sign pressed to the window that said, "Have fun, you two!"

"You arranged this?" Ashlyn asked.

"Just a little something that I've been working on for you and for Zoe."

The mention of Zoe's name paired with hers caused Ashlyn's stomach to flip. Had what she said at the courthouse done something to change his mind?

Ashlyn let him lead her to the van. It was like he had aged backward thirty years. What could have happened in a week's time for such a change to occur? She expected any moment for him to break out skipping. His spirit was so infectiously exuberant, and she was more than curious to see what had caused his transformation.

He opened the side doors and showed her the

wheelchair ramp. "So Zoe can get to her appointments." He closed the doors and opened the passenger side. "Take a ride with me? I promise, you won't be disappointed."

She got in the van and buckled up. Liam ran around the front and hopped in.

"What are you up to? I've never seen you so… cheery. Seriously. You're like a kid on Christmas morning."

"More like someone on Christmas morning expectantly waiting for someone to open the most special gift ever—waiting to see that moment of surprise on their face."

Liam pulled away from Doc's house. Ashlyn looked behind her. The van was roomy. She'd have an easy time maneuvering Zoe's wheelchair. It would make her life so much easier. Surely he didn't mean to gift her this?

"I've been thinking a lot about family and what that means to me," Liam said.

Ashlyn pressed her lips together. "Have you talked with Douglas?"

"That's what I mean. What is the correct definition of that word?"

"I've been thinking a lot about that, too. What conclusion did you come to?"

Liam turned left down the road that would take them to his cabin. "I think family is who you choose to go through life with. It's not all about genetics. You and I both know we didn't do great in that pool of families."

Ashlyn couldn't disagree with him. She remained silent, taking in the surroundings, and tried to pinpoint where some events of Christmas had taken place. She was shuffling through the woods, lugging Emory's baby carrier. Where Liam had tied up the gunman. It looked so different in the daylight gifted with a new perspective. Squirrels ran amok and chittered with one another.

"I've been in therapy," Liam said. "I've only had a few sessions of this... EMDR therapy... but it's already helped so much. My therapist thinks I'm making great progress. I haven't been feeling like I'm drifting away anymore."

Ashlyn shook her head in disbelief. Now she was the one drifting away. It was too much to believe and she placed her hand against the glass, the coolness seeping into her, to connect herself with the present. A switch had been flipped in Liam. This was real. She wasn't dreaming.

When she looked straight ahead, Liam's cabin had changed. A wheelchair ramp had replaced the stairs. A cement path led up to it. Ashlyn stepped out. Her mouth gaped open. "Liam, what have you done?"

He reached for her and placed her hand on the

inside of his elbow. "I've been adding on some necessary items…for our family."

Ashlyn's heart was in her throat. She walked slightly behind him as he led her into the cabin. The shell was the same. The living room with the fireplace. The one bedroom and kitchen. He took her directly to the kitchen table, where there was a scroll of paper. He picked it up and handed it to her.

"What is this?" Ashlyn asked.

"Why would I spoil the fun and tell you before you had the chance to open it?"

Ashlyn's fingers shook and she rolled off the rubber band. She rested the scroll on the table and unrolled it.

It was construction plans.

Ashlyn placed her finger on the things from the blueprint she recognized. The main living room, the kitchen and Liam's bedroom. From there was a hallway that led to a new suite of three rooms.

Liam came up behind her and placed one arm around her waist and nuzzled his face next to hers, resting his chin on her shoulder. She closed her eyes, taking in the moment of his closeness, capturing it for memory. His breath was warm in her ear. His beard tickled her neck, the woodsy scent of his cologne revving her heart more, and then his lips graced her skin with warm and tender kisses from her cheek and then down her neck. She felt his body shift as his other arm came around, and he placed his hand over the top of hers where they rested on the building plans.

"It's an addition," he said, his voice low and sultry in her ear. "For us, for Zoe." He hugged her close. "Open your eyes and look. I'm not going anywhere. I'm not leaving you ever again."

She did as he asked, but she had a hard time focusing through her tears as he moved her finger from place to place, pointing out all the plans he had made to build a special place for them.

"Zoe's bedroom will have a wheelchair accessible bathroom. This new living room will have a great view of the valley. I can't wait to have you decorate it next Christmas. Construction starts as soon as the snow melts."

It was too hard to believe. Ashlyn took her hands, wiped her tears away and turned toward him. "Liam, how can you afford this?"

"I've never spent much money. Invested most of my military earnings. Plus, through some military contacts, I'll be working with a security firm. A lot of celebrities come through here, and they look for protection from someone who knows the area. It's more money than I would have thought possible after leaving the military." He gathered her hands in his. "You can stay here, stay home, and take care of Zoe. You'll be able to meet the judge's demands. Zoe can be with us for always."

Ashlyn leaned into him. *Us*. The two-letter word held so much meaning.

She put her hands on her cheeks, almost pinching herself. Things like this didn't happen to her…to Zoe. A gift like this. A man like Liam.

"There's something you missed," he said and turned her back toward the living room.

He'd redecorated for Christmas. Rid his living room of the paltry, old artificial tree she had decorated. There was a full-bodied pine tree decked out with white Christmas lights and red bulbs. A new cozy gray couch. The fireplace, fully ablaze. Christmas music played in the background. Next to the tree was a pile of wrapped presents. Ashlyn had been so focused on him and his change in persona that she had missed the differences. She inhaled deeply, the smell of pine comforting.

"What else have you done?"

Liam grabbed her hand and laced his fingers through hers. "Come closer and look."

She approached the table next to the tree. On it were wrapped gifts for not only her, but

Doc, Dolores, Mackenzie, Emory…and Zoe. She lightly traced her fingers over the gift tags.

He grabbed a cord and hit a button. New automatic blinds came down over the windows, and the room darkened. That was when she noticed nearly every niche in the room was lit by candlelight.

"Will you join me?" He got onto his knees and motioned her down.

She sat and then lay down, scooting with him under the tree. Not only were the tree lights twinkling, but stars glittered on the ceiling. Ashlyn couldn't help it. She covered her eyes and cried.

Hard, ugly sobs.

He had made plans to construct a place for her and for Zoe. A place she could have never dreamed of. He'd started therapy, gotten a job, so that she could care for Zoe without the pressure of working herself. He was willing to take care of a child that he wasn't biologically connected to. Much like Joseph had on that first Christmas.

He nudged her shoulder. "I think something's stuck in the branches."

Ashlyn pulled her hands down over her nose. Through her tears, the lights starburst. She wiped her eyes. There was a small box with a bow nestled in the under girth. Ashlyn reached up and grabbed it.

She opened it slowly, wanting to savor every moment. That was when she caught a hint of the cinnamon scent. He had truly thought of everything.

Inside, a round-shaped diamond cast off its brilliant light in response to the candles. Liam turned on his side and pulled her close. He laid a hand on her cheek.

"I know you're supposed to do this on one knee, but I wanted to do this under the Christmas tree, where you first showed me how to look at the lights differently. I love you, Ashlyn Sutton. I've loved you for a long time. Your letters were my lifeline. They kept me going through some of the worst years of my life. You are more than I could have hoped for. I think family is who you choose it to be, and I can't imagine building a family without you. Will you marry me?"

Her yes was a kiss.

# EPILOGUE

"Liam, I need your help!"

Liam picked up Zoe and settled her in her wheelchair. He felt the wedding band on his fourth finger—still foreign but treasured. He couldn't believe one month had passed. They'd been married at the cabin one week after his proposal. Once the addition was complete, they would plan something more formal for friends and family. Ashlyn's only request was that it be in the fall.

It was the first celebration in a long time where he wanted to be with other people. A delayed Christmas celebration. His chosen family. None of them biologically related. All of them who he and Ashlyn were going through the rest of this life with. Doc, Dolores, Mackenzie and sweet Emory. Tom Black had been Liam's best man. Mackenzie, the maid of honor. At the beginning, caring for Zoe had felt like he was repaying a debt to the children he couldn't save in Afghanistan. But the more he did it, the more he realized it was a gift for himself. Every time he helped her accomplish something she hadn't been able to do before, the joy in her eyes mended a piece of his broken heart.

"Shall we see what your mother is up to?" he asked Zoe. She nodded and clapped.

The adoption was pending. Liam was training to lead a support group that helped veterans manage and learn to live with PTSD. Who knew there were so many located so close to where he lived?

He pushed Zoe's wheelchair into the living room. Ashlyn looked stunning. Her hair up in a ponytail with tendrils framing her face. Overalls dusted with flour. A smudge of red frosting on her nose. The smell of sugar cookies cooling in the kitchen. Life was simple, warm and sweet.

"How is it you can get Zoe's hair to look so fabulous?" Ashlyn said. "I can't braid it nearly as nice as you can."

"You need gigantic hands for the finer things. It's a well-known secret."

"A well-known secret. You realize that makes little sense, right?" Ashlyn said.

"Everything looks fabulous. I wonder when the last time was that Doc decorated Christmas cookies."

"We're going to have a proper Christmas

celebration. It's time for our tradition." Ashlyn motioned him over, hopping up and down on her feet like a giddy cheerleader. "All of us get under the tree and look at the lights."

He pushed Zoe's wheelchair closer to the tree. "You think we're all going to fit?"

"We won't know unless we try."

Liam scooped up Zoe and laid her gently on the floor. He and Ashlyn scooted under the tree next to her. She raised her hands and batted the lights.

"So pretty!" she exclaimed.

Liam's phone rang. He glanced at the number. It was the county social worker. He took the call, despite Ashlyn's exasperated look.

He listened closely. There was another child. A medically fragile infant that needed foster placement. She couldn't say for how long. It may need to be permanent, considering the circumstances. Liam and Ashlyn had met the requirements to become foster parents for Zoe pending her adoption. The process had been expedited because of Ashlyn's nursing background.

Liam turned to his wife.

"Of course the baby can come here," she said.

"Looks like we need to start that addition sooner than later. Maybe we need to add a few rooms."

\* \* \* \* \*

*If you enjoyed this story, look for these
other books by Jordyn Redwood:*

Fractured Memory
Taken Hostage
Fugitive Spy

Dear Reader,

I cannot tell you how much I love Christmas. Everything about it makes me smile. It gives me great joy to play Christmas music year-round. I'm that person who has multiple Christmas trees decorated—the current count is three, much to my husband's chagrin. I want my house to ooze Christmas spirit.

Christmas is ultimately about gift giving. If we all think back to the genesis that the meaning of Christmas comes from—it is that baby in the manger who grew into our Savior. From Christ's birth story, the image of a baby left on a doorstep and the changes that can happen from that as a novel plot have been on my mind over the years, becoming the story you're reading today.

The medical illness afflicting these children is fictionalized, though the medical basis for the illness is not. There are many genetic diseases that are passed down via the autosomal dominant route, and the points about some diseases expressing differently, penetrance, is true as well. The mRNA vaccines born from the COVID pandemic have given rise to theories about using them to treat various maladies, but none such treatments exist…yet.

I love connecting with readers and would love to hear from you. I can be reached at jordyn@jordynredwood.com or my address: Jordyn Redwood. PO Box 1142. Parker, CO 80134.

Merry Christmas!
*Jordyn*